"You can take the girl now, Marshal, but someone else is going to get her later. That's just how the game's played," Mills shouted.

"What game?" Celeste shouted. "How did you know where I was? Why does Poindexter want me alive?"

"Get in the truck, Celeste," Jonathan said. "Keep your head low. If bullets start flying, gun the engine and don't stop driving until you reach a police station."

He heard the scuff of her footsteps on the snow and the slam of the door closing.

Mills swung back. The gun rose in his hands. His finger flicked over the trigger. Jonathan dropped to one knee and fired, hearing Mills's bullet fly past him a millisecond before his own bullet ripped through the air.

Jonathan leaped in the driver's-side door as Celeste moved over to the passenger side to make room for him.

"Fasten your seat belt and hang on tight!" He glanced at Celeste. "It's going to get rough..."

* * *

Amish Witness Protection

Amish Hideout by Maggie K. Black—January 2019
Amish Safe House by Debby Giusti—February 2019
Amish Haven by Dana R. Lynn—March 2019

Maggie K. Black is an award-winning journalist and romantic suspense author with an insatiable love of traveling the world. She has lived in the American South, Europe and the Middle East. She now makes her home in Canada with her history-teacher husband, their two beautiful girls and a small but mighty dog. Maggie enjoys connecting with her readers at maggiekblack.com.

Books by Maggie K. Black

Love Inspired Suspense

Amish Witness Protection

Amish Hideout

True North Heroes

Undercover Holiday Fiancée
The Littlest Target

True North Bodyguards

Kidnapped at Christmas
Rescue at Cedar Lake
Protective Measures

Killer Assignment
Deadline
Silent Hunter
Headline: Murder
Christmas Blackout
Tactical Rescue

Visit the Author Profile page at Harlequin.com for more titles.

Amish Hideout

Maggie K. Black

HARLEQUIN® LOVE INSPIRED® SUSPENSE

Special thanks and acknowledgment are given to Maggie K. Black
for her contribution to the Amish Witness Protection series.

Recycling programs
for this product may
not exist in your area.

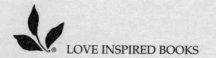

LOVE INSPIRED BOOKS

ISBN-13: 978-1-335-67869-0

Amish Hideout

Copyright © 2018 by Harlequin Books S.A.

www.Harlequin.com

Printed in U.S.A.

He hath made every thing beautiful in his time:
also he hath set the world in their heart,
so that no man can find out the work that
God maketh from the beginning to the end.
—Ecclesiastes 3:11

With thanks to my wonderful agent, Melissa Jeglinski, for her enthusiasm and support, and to my editor, Emily Rodmell, for entrusting me with this story and always pushing me to become a better author. Thanks also to Debby Giusti and Dana R. Lynn, who are writing the next two books in this series. I can't wait to read them.

Finally, thank you to the friend who recently told me off for ignoring who I was with and texting at the dinner table. You were right. Thanks for helping me think about my relationships and how I use my phone in a new way.

ONE

Time was running out for Celeste Alexander. Her sneakered feet tapped on the floor beneath the desk. Her fingers flew over the keyboard so quickly it seemed more like a rapid dance than typing, knowing each keystroke could be her last before US Marshal Jonathan Mast arrived to escort her to her new life in the witness protection program. The early-morning sky lay dark over wintery Pennsylvania farmland outside the safe house window. She knew she should sleep. After all, she had no idea how long the journey ahead would be until she finally reached the small apartment in Pittsburgh that would be her new home for the months until she testified at Dexter Thomes's trial.

It had been almost two weeks since an evil but genius computer hacker, who went by the online handle "Poindexter," had stolen tens of millions of dollars out of the bank accounts of thousands of ordinary Americans in one of the largest bank heists in history, without even leaving his chair. But she'd found him and now he sat in a jail cell, thanks to a single curious thread that Celeste had started following online. When she'd gathered all the evidence she could, she'd tipped off the feds, and Dexter had been arrested. News had quickly spread through the online community that a self-employed computer programmer—a blonde, twenty-six-year-old woman, no less—had uncovered the true identity of the criminal the feds' best minds hadn't been able to find.

But the stolen money still hadn't been recovered. The thought of letting a single one of those people wake up one more day with an empty bank account was unthinkable. Not while there was something she could do about it. She frowned. The battery was down to less than 10 percent and she'd forgotten the charging cable in the room upstairs where she'd slept last night.

"You gave her a laptop?" The voice of US Marshal Stacy Preston came sharply from somewhere behind her. "Please tell me you didn't let her go online. The last thing we need is another misguided Poindexter fan trying to come after her and keep her from testif—"

"Really? You think I joined the service yesterday?" US Marshal Karl Adams shot back even before Stacy had finished her sentence. From what Celeste had seen, those two didn't talk so much as volley sentences back and forth like some kind of verbal tennis match. "Of course not! She had a basic tablet with the internet capability disabled, and after scanning it for bugs, I let her borrow a keyboard."

"And you didn't think to check with me?"

"You were asleep!" Karl said. "Do you check every decision you make with me while you're the one on lookout? It's got zero internet capability. It's not like I gave her a cell phone."

Celeste gritted her teeth, blocked out the verbal sparring of the two US marshals in the room behind her and their sporadic walkie-talkie exchanges with the other marshals positioned around the remote property, and focused her eyes on the text streaming down the screen. Dexter might be in jail. But this would never truly be over. Not until the stolen money was found.

She breathed the prayer and kept typing, ignoring the red low-battery warning. Three days ago, she'd been seconds away from alerting the feds of her crazy suspicion that the unemployed college dropout she'd been digging into online was in fact Poindexter himself, when she'd felt what she thought was God prompting her to first download a complete backup copy of every line of code of his she could see. It had been the right move. By the time the feds broke down his door, Dexter's machines had been wiped clean. But if the feds had found anything in the data she'd recovered, she hadn't heard. Already she could see patterns in the data, though. Many sequences were eight or nine numbers long. Maybe phone numbers and social security numbers? If almost fifteen years of computer programing had taught her anything it was that nothing was ever truly random, no matter how it seemed. In the same way, there was always method and order in what God called her to do. At least, that was how she chose to see it and that was the hope she'd clung to when her apartment went up in a ball of flames.

She'd had no idea just how high a price she'd end up paying when Dexter had shot her a single flippant and cocky message on an online forum about Poindexter's crime. She'd almost ignored it. The online world was a minefield filled with the kind of rude men who seemed to like insulting women for kicks. But something about the glowing way he'd referred to Poindexter in his posts made her suspect he was more than just an admirer of his. So, she'd figured out a way to track him down and followed the right lines of code to prove her hunch was right.

Finding him was the easy part. Getting over her own doubts had been harder. After all, she was a nobody—a freelance computer programmer living on her own in a tiny downtown Philadelphia apartment, taking on small projects while she looked for a full-time job and saved up her pennies to one day move out to the country and have a house of her own. The feds had promised her that she could remain anonymous. But even from behind bars, Dexter had other plans. Within hours of his arrest, her identity had been posted online and her entire nest egg had disappeared from her bank account. Two days later her apartment had exploded just as she'd been steps away from walking through the door. Now, less than twenty-four hours after losing everything but the clothes on her back and the contents of her purse, she sat in a Pennsylvania safe house, clinging to her belief that this was somehow still all part of God's plan for her life.

The two US marshals behind her seemed

to be fiddling with their walkie-talkies. Not that she could make out much of their actual words, just the clicks of them fiddling with the dials and switching channels, and a low murmur of concerned conversation.

"Is everything okay?" Celeste turned and looked over her shoulder, suddenly feeling very aware of her long blond hair as it brushed against her neck and shoulders. Would they make her cut it? Would they make her wear colored contacts to hide the natural green of her eyes? Would she ever be able to go back to writing computer code? Just how much about her life was going to change?

Stacy and Karl exchanged a glance. The pair had been the ones who'd picked her up from the Philadelphia police station and brought her here. Ginger-haired with a lazy grin, Karl's more laid-back attitude had seemed to balance Stacy's more focused approach, despite the fact the there was an odd tension between them, like cats with static electricity. Right now, both of them were frowning.

"Marshal Mast is running late," Stacy said. She brushed her fingers along her temple and tucked a wisp of chestnut hair back into her tight French braid. "We haven't been able to reach him. But at last check-in, Marshal Cormac, who's patrolling the perimeter, reported that nothing seemed off."

"Jonathan's phone probably died." A professional smile brushed Karl's square-jawed face, and Celeste had the distinct impression he was doing it to be reassuring. "He's technophobic, by the way. So whatever you're working on, you'd better get it done before he gets here, because it's possible he'll make you give up the tablet."

He couldn't. Could he? She'd disabled its internet capability herself, and no one had touched it but her and the feds. It was as harmless as a piece of technology could be. The walkie-talkies crackled again. The marshals went back to talking in hushed whispers. She blocked them out, along with that old familiar nagging headache that always started in her temples before slowly spreading through her shoulders and arms until the very tips of her fingers seemed to ache. If US Marshal Jonathan Mast was technophobic, then she'd just have to outrace him and find where Dexter had hidden the money before he got there.

The battery died. She groaned. Well, that was that.

"You guys mind if I go upstairs and get my charging cable? The battery's dead."

The room went black. Then she heard the distant sound of gunfire erupting outside.

"Get Celeste away from the windows!" Karl shouted. "I'll cover the front."

What was happening? *Lord, help us!* Prayers and panic battled in her heart as she felt Stacy's strong hand on her arm pulling her out of her chair and pushing her toward the hallway.

"Stay low and stay close," Stacy said. "We're going to get you out of here."

"No, wait!" Celeste pulled away. "I need the tablet."

The data had been scrubbed from the internet, and the feds were stumped. Leaving without it would mean giving up any hope of finding the money. Wrenching her arm from the marshal's grasp, she reached up and grabbed the tablet, yanking it from the cord and stuffing it inside her sweatshirt.

"Come on!" Stacy shouted. "We have to hurry—"

Her voice was swallowed up in the sound of an explosion, expanding and roaring around them, shattering the windows, tossing Celeste backward and engulfing the living room in smoke. Celeste hit the floor, rolled and hit a door frame. She crawled through it, trying to get away from the smoke billowing behind her. Her eyes stung. The sound of gunfire grew louder. Stacy yelled something about gunmen in the yard. Karl's voice sounded from the darkness telling Celeste to find cover. Her heart beat so hard in her chest she could barely move.

Dexter had found her. Somehow he'd found her in a witness protection safe house. And now he was going to kill her.

Suddenly a strong hand grabbed her out of the darkness, taking her by the arm and pulling her up to her feet so sharply she stumbled backward into a small room. The door closed behind them. She opened her mouth to scream, but a second hand clamped firmly but not unkindly over her mouth. A flashlight flickered on and she looked up through the smoky haze, past worn blue jeans and a leather jacket, to see the strong lines of a firm jaw trimmed with a black beard, a straight nose and, finally, deep and dark, serious eyes staring into hers.

"Celeste Alexander?" He flashed a badge. "I'm Marshal Jonathan Mast. Stay close. I'll keep you safe."

Huge green eyes looked up at him, framed with long dark lashes and wide with fear. Blond hair fell in thick waves around a heart-shaped face. A sweatshirt and faded jeans fell loose over her slender and unmistakably shapely form. He was thankful to see she was wearing shoes and clothes that she could run in. The panicked breath that brushed hot and fast against his palm began to slow. Something stirred deep inside his chest. This was Celeste Alexander? This was the brilliant computer expert that Dexter Thomes would seemingly stop at nothing to keep from testifying at his trial? Of course Jonathan had seen her picture when he'd read her file and picked up the basics: twenty-six, only child, orphaned in college, freelance computer programmer. But somehow it hadn't prepared him for just how beautiful and vulnerable she'd seem.

Help me protect her, Gott.

A prayer crossed his heart so instinctively it shocked him. He couldn't remember the last time he'd prayed for anyone or anything, let alone using the old Pennsylvania Dutch word for "God" from his Amish childhood faith. He and the God of his childhood had been on strict nonspeaking terms since he'd been eighteen, his mother had died and the pain of losing his *mamm* had made him realize he had to choose between the community he came from and the call to serve and protect as a cop. Somehow it had just welled up inside him, taking both his heart and mind by surprise.

He eased his hand away from Celeste's lips. "Are you all right, Miss Alexander?"

"I'm okay, and please call me Celeste," she said, taking a step back and shaking off his hand. Faint tears glittered in the corners of her eyes, and he suspected she was "okay" mostly because she'd decided to be. "Can I call you Jonathan?"

"Sure thing." He nodded, appreciating her directness.

"How did you even know how to find me?" she asked. "I couldn't see a thing."

"I helped my dad evacuate a major barn fire when I was a child," he said. "People and animals. Guess some of it stuck with me."

He wasn't sure why he'd told her that. His childhood was about as comfortable a conversation as his faith was. He'd loved everything about growing up *plain* except for the fact the *Ordnung* guidelines that ordered society made it clear that being Amish and a cop were incompatible. Not that he expected a city-dwelling computer programmer to feel anything but disdain or amusement at a life without technology. But, judging by the way her shoulders relaxed, it seemed to set her at ease. "Did everyone make it out alive? From the barn fire?"

"Yes, they did." A slight and unexpected grin brushed his lips. "Even the barn cats. And I'm going to get you out of here alive and safely now. When did you get here?"

"Last night." Those compelling eyes grew wider.

He frowned. He disliked informing a subject of too much of an operation, but the walkie-talkies were down and she had information he needed. Hopefully, she was as levelheaded as her file had led him to believe.

"On my way here I got an email from Marshal Karl Adams telling me that there was a change of plans and you weren't arriving until tomorrow," he said. The rise of her brows told him in an instant how right he'd been to suspect something was up. "It told me to turn around and go home. But I decided to proceed. As I got closer, I saw a black SUV parked by the road ahead and no one was answering the walkie-talkie. So I called for backup and hid my vehicle, then cut through the woods and came in through an underground tunnel entrance. How many hostiles have you seen?"

"None," she said. "I just saw the explosion and heard gunfire. I was with Stacy and Karl in the living room and then the windows exploded. There was just so much smoke and gunfire I barely knew which way was up. We need to make sure they're okay. I really don't think Karl sent that email. He seems pretty straight up. They both do. I suspect someone hacked his email and also jammed the walkie-talkies."

She was probably right about Karl. In fact, Karl's casual openness about his Christian faith had the irritating habit of reminding Jonathan how much he missed his own.

"Well, if you can get me to the walkie-talkie jammer, I can disable it so you can be back in communication with your team."

Her chin rose. He blinked. He was here to protect her. She was the one in danger and she was offering to help him?

"Agents Preston and Adams are well trained and dedicated, as are the other marshals on-site," he said. Without a doubt they were all currently risking their lives to find and protect Celeste. "Contacting them and letting them know you're all right will be my top priority, once I've got you to safety. Right now, all that matters is getting you out of here alive. Follow me and I'll take you out the way I came in."

He switched off the flashlight and waited

for his eyes to adjust. One of the benefits of growing up *plain* was that he'd always known the darkness as a friend to be embraced and not an enemy to be combatted with a glare of electric lights. Sunrise was less than twenty minutes away. He needed to get her into his truck before then. He eased the door open a crack and listened. Gunfire sounded in intermittent bursts from somewhere else on the property. Smoke seeped down the hall, but he neither felt nor heard flames. It had been a small explosive device, he imagined, just intended to take out the front door and windows, making it easier to breach the building.

He steadied himself to lead her down the hall to freedom, but instead felt the furtive brush of her hand on his arm. "I need to go back to my room. It's upstairs."

"I'm sorry, there isn't time." He didn't turn. "But there's a bag of spare winter clothes hidden in the passage and more necessities in my truck."

"But I need a charger for my tablet—"

"No, you don't. You shouldn't be on the grid at all."

Again Jonathan readied himself to go. This time her hand tightened on his arm.

"I wasn't planning on going 'on the grid.' I

need to review some of Dexter Thomes's data while completely off the grid, and until I can get my tablet charged, it's dead."

Something as strong as iron moved through her voice. Even in the dim light he could see the firm jut of her shoulders. He remembered looking at her file and wondered how anyone—let alone a well-meaning citizen—could possibly have the patience and determination to sit at a computer for eighteen hours chasing down a criminal hacker. Now he was beginning to see. "The feds have people chasing the money. All you need to focus on is staying alive long enough to testify."

Gunfire erupted somewhere to their right. He could hear the voices of US marshals shouting. Sounded like hostiles were about to breach the house. Then he heard a familiar voice coming down the hall. He stepped through the door, keeping Celeste safely behind him.

"Karl!" he called, relief filling his chest as his eyes fell on the familiar form. "I have Celeste! I'm taking her out through the underground passage. I've called for backup and I'll get in touch once we're safe."

"Thank You, God," Karl prayed. He said, "You're a sight for sore eyes. We have four hostiles on the perimeter. Stacy is holding down the front door. Communication's down." Gunfire grew louder. Stacy's voice echoed through the darkness, calling for Karl. "Stay safe."

"You, too."

Karl turned and ran toward the front of the house. Jonathan reached for Celeste's hand, enveloped it in his and ran down the hallway. They pushed through a door into a large country kitchen. He closed the door behind them, then glanced down at the woman whose small hand had slid so naturally into his. He dropped her hand, an odd heat rising to his face. Now why had he done that? They started across the kitchen floor toward the cellar. Suddenly the door behind them flew back. A thin man in a dark ski mask burst through with a gun in his grasp. Celeste screamed. The man set her in his sights and fired. But Jonathan had thrown himself between Celeste and the gunman before the bullet could meet its mark. They tumbled to the ground as he heard the bullet strike the wall behind them.

Jonathan rolled up to one knee and returned fire. The gunman fell back behind the door. "Celeste! Get behind the counter and stay low!"

Jonathan gritted his teeth and braced his hand against the wooden floorboards. There was no way to reach the cellar now, not without running straight into the line of fire. Even if they managed to make it, they'd tip the criminal off about where they were going and there'd be nothing to stop him from following. He'd spent the first eighteen years of his life in a huge country kitchen like this one and now he was going to die in one, trying to protect a woman he'd barely met and yet who had already managed to tug at strings he hadn't even known he had. Another bullet flew through the kitchen door, shredding the corner of the countertop and sending wood chips flying. Suddenly he knew their way out.

"Celeste! There's a pantry behind you. Crawl inside and wait for me there."

"Got it!" She started crawling, and he followed, keeping low to the ground. They reached the pantry and slipped inside. He closed the door behind them and pushed a shelf against it.

"Now, stand back," he said. She pressed her back against the wall, whispered words tumbling from her lips. The tension in his heart tightened to realize she was praying, and when he spoke again his voice felt oddly husky in his throat. "Don't worry. Everything's going to be okay. There's more than one way into the cellar."

He holstered his weapon, bent down and felt with his fingers along the floorboards. Then he pulled out his pocketknife and slid the blade between the head of one of the loosest nails and the well-worn wood. Within moments he'd worked it free. He moved on to the next. All he had to do was remove two boards and that should be enough for them to slip through. Voices shouted in the kitchen beyond them. Sounded like the gunman had been joined by a second. He worked the board loose and pried it back. Then he grabbed the one beside it and yanked it off, as well. A hole lay at their feet. It was a crude means of escape and once someone checked the pantry it would be clear where they'd gone, but hopefully it would buy them enough time to get a head start.

"I'm going to jump down now," he said. "It's only about eight feet. When I call you I need you to jump in after me and I'll catch you. Okay? Trust me. I'll keep you safe."

He reached for her again. He felt her fingers slide between his and squeeze. Then he pulled away.

"Ready?" he asked. She nodded. He dropped through the hole and tumbled into darkness.

TWO

Celeste crouched by the hole and waited for Jonathan to give her the all clear. There was a scuffling sound beneath her like something falling. Then there was silence. The kitchen door slammed back on its hinges. Loud footsteps sounded as a second person stormed into the room.

"She ran in here!" It was a male voice, raspy and hoarse.

"And you opened fire?" A second male voice let out a string of swear words. This voice was cold and sharp, like the sound of a knife slicing through wood. "What are you doing? I need her alive!"

Alive. Something about that one simple word and the menace with which it was delivered made her limbs shake. She bent down lower, bracing her quaking hand against the wood, waiting for the sound of Jonathan's words telling her it was safe to jump.

Lord, You've been my light and my guide no matter how rocky things got. Please guide me now.

"Where did she go?" The commanding voice was back.

"I don't know!"

Then came the sharp beam of light swinging back and forth in the dim kitchen, sending sudden bursts of glaring white light shining through the gap between the door and the door frame, blinding her eyes for a moment before swinging around the kitchen again. She peered out through the tiny gap. The man who'd been shooting at them had rolled up his ski mask. Not much, but enough for her to see he was grizzled, probably in his early sixties, with the kind of broken nose that had been punched more than once and a scar down one side of his jaw, breaking up the gray-and-white stubble.

"Well, find her! I'm not paying for nothing!"

Paying? Who was this second man? Why did he need her alive? What did he think he was paying for?

"I'm ready for you! Time to jump." Jonathan's voice floated up through the hole.

She hesitated. She needed to see that man's face. Just for a moment. She needed to know who was giving the instructions and who Dexter Thomes had sent after her.

"Come on!" Jonathan's voice grew firmer. "We've got to go."

She stretched her legs slowly, her hand inching up the door frame as she slowly got to her feet. She could see the man's legs now, clad in jeans and a dark jacket. Shaggy brown hair fell around his shoulders. He wasn't wearing any kind of mask, almost like he wanted his face to be seen.

Just one glance. That was all she needed. Just a little bit more data to complete the picture.

"Celeste!" Jonathan hissed. Urgency strained the marshal's voice. "Hurry up!"

The figure turned. She recoiled, wondering for a moment if he'd somehow managed to hear Jonathan's whisper above the ruckus of gunfire and shouting outside. The man's eyes seemed to lock on her hiding place and suddenly she saw his face, with its shaggy beard, blue-tinted glasses and squinting eyes.

She stumbled backward. No... No, it couldn't be.

He raised a finger, then started toward the cupboard. She took another step back. Her foot slipped and she fell. She bit her lip and barely kept from screaming as air rushed past her.

Then she felt the strength of Jonathan's arms around her breaking her fall. She gasped a prayer of thanksgiving. Darkness filled her gaze. The smell of damp earth and old brick rushed in with each breath. For a moment silence fell, punctuated only by the sound of Jonathan's ragged breath. "Are you all right? What happened?"

No, she wasn't all right and she couldn't begin to make sense of what she'd seen.

"Do you know if they saw where you went or where you were hiding?" he asked. But somehow her mouth couldn't form words. It was like her brain was stuck on just one thought. Dexter Thomes. She'd seen Dexter... Jonathan's hand brushed her elbow and steered her down the tunnel. "We've got to move. Come on."

He marched her down the hallway. Her footsteps faltered beneath her.

It couldn't be Dexter. He'd been arrested—he was behind bars awaiting trial, and if he'd escaped or been released someone would've told her. If he was on the run, would he actually be brazen enough to walk into a witness protection safe house without even covering his face? There was something chilling about the arrogance of a man who'd go by a moniker Poindexter that was so close to his own first name. But all of her research had shown he was an only child. He didn't have a twin…

She opened her mouth, but no words came out, and, instead, a long shiver spread through her body.

"Don't worry, I have a bag of warm clothes and supplies hidden up ahead," Jonathan said.

Her limbs were shaking all right, but it wasn't from the cold. She had to tell him what she'd seen. "Listen, after you jumped through the hole in floor, I heard the gunfire stop and two men talking. I listened to what they were saying and tried to get a look at them—"

"That's not your job," he said. "Your job is staying alive, and when I give you an instruction, I expect you to follow it. Now come on."

"Wait, it's important…"

"Tell me later. When we're out of this tunnel and somewhere safe."

Yes, but if it really was Dexter in the kitchen and he came after them, shouldn't Jonathan arrest him? Shouldn't someone do something?

"Wait, I think it was Dexter!" If he heard her, he gave no indication, and he was propelling her at such a brisk walk that she was almost jogging to keep up with his long stride. "He said he wanted me alive."

"It doesn't matter if Dexter sent him or not." His pace didn't even falter. "All that matters is that I'm going to keep you safe."

She nearly growled. Was he always this pigheadedly focused? She stopped so short he seemed to barely catch himself from tripping over her. "No, listen, I mean, I think it was literally Dexter Thomes. I just saw Dexter Thomes—Poindexter himself—or a very good lookalike standing in the kitchen, barking orders and talking about taking me alive."

Jonathan felt his mouth open and shut like a trout. He wasn't used to being caught off guard and didn't much like it. He ran a hand over the back of his neck. "That's impossible. Dexter Thomes is in jail. I don't know how you could even tell in the ski mask."

"He wasn't wearing one and the other man pulled his up while they were talking." Even in the dim light he could tell her arms had crossed. "And I'm telling you that either Dexter, or a doppelgänger who looks remarkably a lot like him, is barking orders upstairs."

Right. Well, he didn't know what that meant, but thankfully it didn't sound like anyone was coming down the tunnel after them, at least for now. Had they not checked the cupboard? Had they been distracted by something?

"I know Dexter Thomes better than anyone," she continued. "I did my homework before reporting him to the feds. He's an only child. He doesn't have a sibling or a twin. He shouldn't be out on parole…"

Her words paused as his hand brushed her shoulder. "I hear what you're saying and as soon as we're safe and clear I'm going to call my boss, Chief Deputy Louise Hunter, for an update and I'll tell her what you said."

"I want to tell her myself."

"Fine." He hadn't expected someone who sat behind a computer all day to be quite so driven and tenacious. "Now we need to keep moving."

He pulled a flashlight from his belt and switched it on. His eyes didn't exactly need the light to see and it ran the risk of alerting anyone who was following them, but for now they seemed to be alone. Celeste was clearly rattled, and he had a hunch it would make her more comfortable. He swung the beam over the old red-and-orange brick walls and then tilted it down to illuminate the path ahead of their feet. He started jogging again, fast enough to keep moving but not so fast he couldn't detect any danger ahead. She kept pace.

"You said it didn't matter if he wanted me dead or alive," she said, after a long moment. "But of course it matters. When you're analyzing data you can't ignore anything. Not the fact he wanted me alive. Not the fact one of them looked exactly like Dexter Thomes and the other like a sixty-something criminal enforcer."

Wow, she didn't let up, did she? Her legs might be struggling to keep up with his long strides, but that was nothing compared to what she was doing to his brain. "So, you heard a man who looked like Dexter Thomes tell a violent thug in his sixties that he wanted you alive?"

"Correct."

"And I'm telling you, it doesn't matter what he said."

"How can you say it doesn't matter?"

"Because who's to say he was telling the truth?" His voice rose, and he winced as he heard it echo off the tunnel walls. Thankfully, it seemed they weren't being followed, because if the flashlight hadn't alerted them the sound of their voices would have. "He's a criminal! He might've said he was going to keep you alive and then kill you anyway.

You can't predict what a monster like that is going to do."

"Dexter Thomes isn't a monster—he's a man," Celeste argued. "A very smart, evil and cunning man who spent years planning his heist. Everything he does matters. Even the fact that either he didn't check the cupboard to see if I was in there, or he saw the hole and decided not to come down after me." Huh. So she'd noticed that, too. "My life is staring at tiny pieces of code and lines of text, looking for the patterns. That's how I found him and that's how I'm going to find the money he stole. That's who I am. I'm a computer programmer."

Something almost like understanding flickered in the corner of his mind, but he didn't let it take root. A chill brushed his skin. Cold air was seeping in from somewhere. Was the door to the entrance open?

"And I'm a US marshal with the Federal Witness Protection Program," he said. "I place witnesses into new lives and keep them safe. Maybe one day you'll go back to being a computer programmer again, but right now, you're a witness. Now, we need to stop talking, and if anything happens stay behind me."

His footsteps slowed. He needed to figure out where the cold was coming from. Celeste fell into step beside him and he had the unexpected and ridiculous urge to slide his arm around her shoulder. Instead, he switched off his flashlight, keeping one hand on it and the other on his holstered weapon. Their feet moved without making a sound. He'd never minded quiet. In fact, he preferred it over noise. But there was nothing comfortable or peaceful about the bubble of silence that surrounded Celeste. She was on edge and uneasy. It was like her mind was a whirling machine, spinning and turning so quickly her entire body radiated tension. His hand twitched with the desire to brush his fingers reassuringly across her shoulder blades and tell her that she had nothing to worry about, because he was here and he would keep her safe.

Faint and pale light trickled through from the end of the tunnel.

"Stay here," he said. "As close to the wall as you can get. I mean it. Don't move. Don't go anywhere."

"Got it! I'll stay right here with my back against the wall." Her voice was almost defiant, then suddenly her tone dropped and he felt a hand brush his arm. "I'm sorry about what happened earlier. I didn't mean to make your job any harder that it already is."

He swallowed. "It's okay. It can't be easy

to go from being a folk hero to thousands of people to taking orders from someone like me. Now, wait here. I'll be back in a second."

He pulled away from her and walked slowly and carefully down to the end of the tunnel. Something lay across the doorway. His heart stopped.

It was the body of a US marshal.

THREE

"Stand back!" Jonathan's voice echoed down the tunnel ahead of her. Celeste's heart pounded hard in her chest as she heard the worry moving through his deep voice.

Dear Lord, was I wrong to stay up above in the kitchen and listen? Did I really see who I thought I saw? What can I do? How can I help? I feel so helpless.

She'd felt almost fearless days ago when she was sitting in her living room, alone with her laptop searching for Poindexter. She'd never expected to be able to find him. Not really. She'd just started pulling one thread that led to another thread and then another, until they reached deeper and deeper into Poindexter's online web to the man in the center of it all. But no, she hadn't felt like a hero. She hadn't even figured out where he'd hid the money. Besides, all she'd been doing was using her talent to the best of her ability and counting on God to guide her.

"What's going on?" she called.

At first there was no sound except the beat of her own heart. Then she heard a deep, long sigh moving through the darkness.

"Hang on one second," Jonathan said. "There's a body here. It's another marshal by the look of it. I need a moment to check it out and also do a visual sweep for any hostiles. I need you to stay there and don't move until I give you the all clear. Please confirm that you've heard me."

"I've heard you," she said. She pressed her back against the wall, feeling the cold of the bricks seep into her limbs. She wasn't cut out for this. She didn't hide in dark tunnels. In fact, she rarely even left her little rented apartment in the city, not that she didn't love the thought of country living. In fact, thanks to the internet she'd been able to shop for handmade clothes and blankets from self-employed seamstresses, handmade soaps from home-based artisans and order everything imaginable—from fresh vegetables grown on farms outside the city to homemade soups to cheeses, breads and even pies. Before someone working for Dexter had emptied her bank account and wrecked her credit, she'd been saving up for years to buy an actual house of her own, somewhere outside the city, where grass and trees would fill her view from the window beside her desk instead of buildings and buses. She'd lost all of that; she was trapped. She pressed her hands to her eyes to keep sudden tears at bay.

Lord, I know I should trust You have a plan in all this. I've trusted You to guide me this far. I need to believe You won't abandon me now.

Then she heard Jonathan's voice again, deep, comforting and as solid as steel.

"Celeste? A US marshal has been shot and killed. His name was Rod Cormac. He was a good man. My guess is he was shot at a distance and tried to make it to the safe house to warn the rest of the team before he died. He didn't look like he was followed. Now I need you to come to me, nice and slow."

She took a step forward and saw them. Jonathan was crouched down on the ground beside the body of a man, lit by the soft gray light of the approaching dawn. The man's hair was blond and his limbs were curled up like he'd just lain down to have a nap in the snow. Her body froze. She couldn't move. She couldn't do this. She wasn't cut out for any of it.

"Look at me, Celeste," Jonathan said firmly. "Don't look at him. Look at me."

His voice was a soft-spoken command, snapping her eyes back to his face, and if she was honest with herself, there was something almost kind of comforting about it. He held her gaze every bit as firmly as if it was her hand inside his. "It's going to be okay, and I will keep you safe. Just trust me and do what I say. Okay?"

She nodded. He broke her gaze and reached for something in the shadows by the wall. It was a large black bag. He pulled out a gray wool blanket and laid it carefully over the body. Then he knelt for one long moment beside the fallen marshal. Jonathan's head bowed, his eyes closed and his lips moved in what she could only guess was silent prayer. A shudder moved through his limbs. Then he stood and wiped his hand over his eyes.

He pulled out a thick coat and tossed it to her as he stood. "Put this on. There should be gloves and a hat in the pockets. We'll find you winter boots as soon as we can. We need to hurry. It's only a matter of time before someone finds the blood trail and follows him here."

Celeste looked down at the coat in her

hands but somehow couldn't get her arms to move. Then her gaze rose to the snow-covered trees beyond the doorway. What if the person who'd shot Rod was still out there? What if they got shot the moment they stepped through the door? A man she'd never met was dead. And why? Because she'd hacked some lines of computer code and was going to be a witness at the criminal's trial? Right now, Stacy, Karl and several other marshals were fighting for their lives because of her. Someone had already died because of her, and there was no way of knowing how many more would before this was all done. The horror of that welled up inside her.

Jonathan stepped forward, gently took the coat from her hands and held it out for her to slide her arms into. Her eyes met his for one long moment, and her breath caught to see the depth of sorrow echoed there.

"What was he like?" she asked. She let him ease her hands into the sleeves.

"Rod was a good marshal and a good man." Something in the tone of his voice made her think this wasn't the first colleague he'd lost in the line of duty. "He had a wacky sense of humor. I liked working with him."

She felt him slide the coat up over her

shoulders. She didn't know why she was so frozen or why her body didn't want to move, only that asking questions somehow helped. "Did he have a family?"

"He had a very large black dog and a very nice long-term girlfriend who he never tied the knot with because this line of work involves a lot of travel and doesn't lend itself to relationships."

He nudged her shoulder. She looked up into his face.

"How exactly did he die? Don't just say he was shot. I want to understand."

"He was shot twice in the abdomen," Jonathan said. His tone was steady and without a hint of uncertainty. There was something comforting about it. "He lost a lot of blood and passed out."

She bit her lip. "Did he suffer?"

He paused, then reached down and slowly helped her do her zipper up.

"I won't lie. He would've been in a lot of pain. But he also used his dying breath and the last ounce of energy he had to get here. My guess is that he was trying to warn us about what was happening and tell us there were hostiles on the property. When backup arrives they'll retrieve the body and notify his family. He died a hero's death and will get a hero's funeral. Now we have to move. Come on."

Still, she was hesitating. She needed more answers.

"I don't understand why the person in the kitchen looked like Dexter—if he's really in jail," she said. "Or why he wants me alive. Or why the walkie-talkies were down or how anyone could find a WITSEC safe house. I don't even know if Karl and Stacy and all the other US marshals protecting me are going to be okay. What if there are more shooters in those trees? What if they shoot at us? What if they kill you and take me?"

Her voice rose to a wail, and as much as she hated it she didn't know how to get control of it again. Her hands began to shake, a harsh uncontrollable quivering that moved up her arms and into her body.

"Celeste!" Jonathan's voice grew urgent. "Focus. Look at me. You're in shock. It's totally understandable, but you've got to fight through it. Now I don't know how computers work. I've never opened one up and looked inside, and you could definitely say I didn't exactly grow up in a technologically advanced house. But I'm guessing that in computer code every character or number has a purpose, right? Every part has its own thing it's doing? Right?"

She blinked and a smile crossed her face, which was so unexpected it shocked her. What an odd way to explain it. He wasn't right, but kind of close. "Something like that."

"Okay," he said. "Well, each of us has a job to do. Rod's was to watch the perimeter. Karl and Stacy's job is to hold down the fort and give us a chance to get out of here." He took another step toward her. His hands rested on her shoulders. "Your job is to testify against the man who's ultimately responsible for Rod's death and make sure he faces justice for stealing all those people's money. And my job is to keep you safe until you do."

He stood there a moment with his hands on her shoulders, and something inside her wanted to step closer, to lean into his chest and let his strong arms envelop her, in a way no man had since her father had died. Even though she barely knew Jonathan Mast, and he didn't seem like the type who was into hugs. She closed her eyes and felt her lips move in silent prayer. The she opened her eyes, swallowed hard and stepped back. "Okay, I'm ready to go."

She grabbed a pair of leather gloves from the pocket of her coat and pulled them on.

He did the same from his. He reached for her hand. She took it and he quickly yet carefully led her around the body and out into the cold predawn air. They ran, pressing through the thick trees as their feet pounded down the snow. The ground sloped beneath their feet. Gunfire echoed in the distance. The sun was starting to rise as the faintest pink sliver of light along the gray horizon. The trees parted and she saw the road.

Jonathan dropped her hand and led her along the tree line to where a large and tough-looking truck lay hidden in the trees by a camouflage cover. "Stand way back. I need a minute to uncover the truck, do a quick sweep to make sure no one tampered with it, and get it back on the road. Then we're good to go."

She crossed over to the other side of the road and waited as he started the engine and slowly pulled the truck back onto the road. A small battered-looking car flew down the road to her left and fishtailed to a stop. A tall heavyset young man behind the wheel held a cell phone.

"Hey! I think we've found her! Start recording!" a shorter and stockier young man called, leaping out of the passenger side. Celeste turned and ran, sprinting in the direction of Jonathan's truck. A blast sounded in the air behind her. She stopped and turned back. The young man's shoulders rolled back in a swagger as he pointed a handgun sideways at her. "Yo, you're Celeste, right? Celeste Alexander? You're that hacker chick that Poindexter's got a bounty out on? I'm Miller. That there with the phone recording, this is my buddy, Lee. Get in the car now! Or I'll kill ya!"

Jonathan shifted into Drive and was about to punch the engine when one word he'd heard the thugs shout a split second earlier finally caught up with his brain. *Recording.* The brazen thugs now pointing a gun at Celeste weren't just announcing their crime like a bad online video—they were recording it, too. Just like whoever Celeste had seen in the kitchen they weren't wearing ski masks. No, these two wanted to be both seen and known.

Thankfully, Jonathan was wearing civilian clothing. He shoved a hat down hard over his head and wrapped a scarf around his face. Then he gunned the engine. The truck shot out of the woods and straight across the road, swerving to a stop behind Celeste so that the driver's side door was directly behind her.

She spun back, her eyes wide. Her hand rose to her lips.

The gun-wielding showman jumped back in shock with a shout that turned into a nervous laugh. "Whoa! Lee, you getting this? Make sure you're getting this!"

Jonathan unholstered his weapon. Disgust whelmed up inside him. These criminals were threatening Celeste at gunpoint and treating it as some kind of game, when a good man had just died protecting her. He leaped from the truck and raised his gun high with both hands. "Celeste! Get behind me!"

She ran for him, darting behind him so quickly she nearly slid and fell. Miller turned back.

"Who are you?" Miller shouted. Jonathan didn't answer. No, he wasn't about to announce who he was and flash his badge on camera until he found out what exactly they were caught up in. For now, being undercover suited him just fine. Miller jabbed the air with the barrel of his gun. "Look, I don't want trouble. I just want the hacker girl. Let me take her and go."

His voice shook. There was a whole lot of nervousness hiding behind the bravado, and desperation, too. Not that it made anyone safer. A determined and reckless amateur was every bit as dangerous as a professional.

"That's not going to happen," Jonathan shouted. "Put the gun down."

Miller waited a long moment, eyeing him as if weighing invisible options. Jonathan stared him down and didn't blink. The US marshal had no doubt what would happen if it came to a shoot-out, but still he was going to do anything in his power to stop it from happening. He could still remember vividly what it was like to fire a gun for the first time. For a young man coming from an Amish background, there'd been something so foreign about it. Now, as his eyesight narrowed, his shoulders relaxed and his fingers prepared to fire, it was as comfortable as if the weapon was an extension of him. He just prayed that today wouldn't be the first day he took a life in the line of duty.

"Whatever, man!" Miller threw his hands up like an exaggerated shrug. "You win this round. I don't care. I'm just in it for the money, and Lee here's just got us probably a grand's worth of footage. Poindexter's got everyone with dark web access and the willingness to step up and make a few bucks out looking for her. So, you can take her now, but someone else is going to take her back from you later. That's just how the game's played."

"What game?" Celeste's voice came from

behind Jonathan. "Tell me! How did you know where I was? Why does Poindexter want me taken alive?"

Miller didn't answer. Instead, he turned back toward the car, gun still dangling from his fingers as he had a quick word with Lee outside of Jonathan's earshot.

"Get in the truck," Jonathan said without turning. "Keep your head low. The keys are in the ignition. If bullets start flying, gun the engine and don't stop driving until you reach a police station."

Please, Celeste, don't argue with me. He heard the scuffle of her footsteps on the snow and the slam of the door closing. *Thank You, Gott!*

Miller nodded to Lee. Then he swung back. The gun rose in his hands. His finger flicked over the trigger. Jonathan dropped to one knee and fired, hearing Miller's bullet fly past him into the trees a millisecond before his own bullet ripped through the arm now pointing a gun at him. Miller dropped the gun, grabbing his arm and collapsing to the ground as a scream flew from his lips. Lee turned his camera phone toward his writhing partner.

Jonathan bounded into the driver's side as Celeste moved over to the passenger side to make room for him. He holstered his weapon, shut the door and slammed his seat belt on in one seamless move.

"Fasten your seat belt and hang on tight!" He glanced at Celeste. "It's going to get rough."

FOUR

He heard her seat belt click. Jonathan's truck surged backward, coming within a foot of hitting Miller before swerving sharply off the road to get around the criminals' car. For a split second the entire scene played out before him in a glance. A howling and angry young man was down on the ground beside the car. Another bullet ripped from his gun that once again failed to meet its mark. The second young man bounded from the car and ran toward Miller, filming the scene with his phone as he did, and somehow Jonathan's eyes managed to meet his and hold them for a split second. They were devoid of emotion. This wasn't personal. It was just a payday for whatever criminal found her first. How was he supposed to protect Celeste against that?

Then he threw the truck into Drive.

"Hold on!" he shouted. "We're about to spin!"

He hit the gas and yanked the steering

wheel hard to the right. The truck spun. Its wheels skimmed over the ice. He waited until the final moment, and tapped the breaks and yanked the wheel back. The truck righted. They sped forward, down the road as trees and the early-dawn sky flew past them in a blur of white, pale purples and grays. Gunshots faded in the distance. The sun crept over the edge of the horizon. He pulled off the scarf and hat, then glanced at Celeste. "Are you okay?"

Her smile was weak, but she seemed to be giving it her best shot. "That was some driving. Guessing you must've been tearing up the streets when you were a teenager."

He shifted his gaze to the windshield ahead. The road spread ahead of him in an endless line of white. "Actually, I didn't get my license until I was twenty."

Before then it had just been horses driving the family buggy. It was funny. As a teenager, he couldn't wait to get behind the wheel of a car and drive. But when he had, he'd been surprised how impersonal it felt. It didn't listen or respond. It was just a machine, like any other.

"Speaking of vehicles, our first stop is going to be switching this truck out for another one," he said. "I do use the other truck when I can because it drives better. But the fact Lee was recording all that makes it more important that we do. Then it's about a five-hour drive to the new safe house, which, as I believe you know, is set in an apartment complex in the suburb of Pittsburgh. We'll stop for breakfast in about an hour, but there are some granola bars, apples and bottles of water in the cooler behind your seat. I've got to call my supervisor and let her know where we're at."

He reached for his earpiece, clipped it to his ear and turned on his phone. Celeste's fingers brushed his arm.

"Wait, aren't we first going to talk about what happened?" she asked.

He sat back. "I don't know what went wrong, how those criminals found you or what they're really after. Clearly, someone's out to get you and trolling to rope in any criminal element they can find, from people with tactical weapons and smoke bombs, to idiots with cell phones. Hopefully, talking to my supervisor will help."

He dialed the number.

"Louise Hunter." His supervisor's voice came on the line, crisp and clear. He had no idea how old Chief Deputy Hunter was, but both the streaks of gray in her jet-black hair and the stories she told led him to believe she was probably hovering somewhere on either side of sixty. She was the kind of woman who'd been married to the same man for forty years, had fourteen grandchildren and a career that spanned countless escaped convicts, national manhunts and hundreds of lives saved.

Jonathan gave her a heads-up that Celeste was sitting beside him in the truck and then filled her in on Rod Cormac's death and the ambush at the safe house. As much as he hated briefing his boss in front of the person he was assigned to protect, time was of the essence and there weren't that many options. Then she confirmed what he'd feared—this was the first update she'd received about the situation at the safe house since he himself had called for backup before going to find Celeste. Communications were still down at the farm. He could only hope Stacy and Karl were okay.

"Rod was a dedicated marshal," Hunter said. "He'll be deeply missed." There was a pause, long enough to let him know she felt the sudden loss every bit as hard as he did. "Unfortunately, we haven't been able to confirm anything about the situation or the safety of the other marshals on-site. But we have a team currently moving into formation. I will make sure you are updated as soon as we have more information. How is Miss Alexander doing?"

Jonathan glanced over at Celeste. Her head was turned away from him. The morning rays caught her golden hair.

"Miss Alexander is safe and well. She was thankfully unharmed and has come through her ordeal with remarkable resilience," he said. Was *remarkable* too strong a word? Perhaps. But it was true. "She'd like to speak to you personally about the man she saw in the safe house. She said he looked like Dexter Thomes."

"I'd like to speak to her, as well," said Hunter.

He reached to turn off his earpiece, then paused. "Are we certain that Dexter Thomes is still behind bars?"

"Last I heard," she said. "But I will be confirming that immediately."

"Thank you." He kept one hand on the steering wheel. With the other he switched off the earpiece and then he held out the phone toward his passenger. "Celeste, my supervisor, Chief Deputy Louise Hunter, would like to speak to you. I've switched off my earpiece, so her voice should come through the phone's speaker now. But if not, I'm sure you know how to change that in the settings."

"Thank you." Her fingers brushed his, just briefly, as he handed her the phone and he felt something like electricity rush through him.

What was it about this woman that had this strange impact on him? Her file had been thin. Her parents had died when she'd been just nineteen, and had no siblings and no significant romantic entanglements. She'd taught herself programming in elementary school and won several computer, electronic and robotic awards in high school and university. She'd started getting a master's degree but had to drop out for financial reasons and had made her own way as a self-employed computer programmer after having been turned down for way too many tech jobs that she was clearly overqualified for.

Brilliant and attractive, not to mention tenacious, it was no wonder he was attracted to her. He could rationalize that much at least. But, even if circumstances had been different, she deserved better than a man like him who, when faced with a choice between the career he felt called to and his own family and Amish heritage, had walked away and chosen work because the call on his heart to serve his country had been too loud for him to ignore.

Yes, he'd been eighteen, Mamm had just died, his older *bruder* and only sibling had told him he had to make a choice, and his *pa* had never been someone he'd felt like he could talk to. But it had been his choice and one he could never undo. He shuddered to think what a woman who had no family would ever think of a man who'd walked away from his.

He took a deep breath, pushed aside the unwanted thoughts and listened as she talked to Hunter. Truth was, he wasn't sure what to expect. After all, she'd been pretty stubborn back at the safe house and dug her heels in pretty hard. To his surprise she was crisp, polite and thorough, going through exactly what she'd heard and seen without any embellishments or exaggerations.

"The man I saw looked exactly like Dexter Thomes," she told Hunter, "even though my vantage point was obscured by smoke and low light. Clearly, if Dexter is still in prison, he must be a doppelgänger, but the similarity was uncanny. I researched everything I could find about Dexter Thomes before I contacted the feds and told them my suspicions he was Poindexter. His mother is deceased, his father is not listed on his birth certificate and he has no known siblings. If he had a secret twin I should've uncovered it."

The women exchanged a few more words, and he noticed Celeste made a point of asking his boss to please let them know when the safe house had been secured and if the other marshals were all right. Then she handed the phone to Jonathan. He switched his earpiece back on.

"I'd like you to take her to the central Pennsylvania safe house outside of Altoona for one night," Hunter said, "while we do another sweep of the Pittsburgh apartment and also confirm that Dexter Thomes is really still behind bars. Barring any unforeseen difficulties, she can move into the Pittsburgh apartment tomorrow."

"Understood," he nodded, feeling the lines of a frown wrinkle his forehead. The plan would add extra travel time and delay the start of her new identity and life. Not to mention the diversion would take them right through Amish country and painfully close to the family farm he'd left behind. He thanked his boss and they ended the call.

"Everything okay?" Celeste asked.

"I hope so," he said. "She'll keep us posted. We're going to take a brief detour to another safe house for one night and then head on to your new apartment in Pittsburgh tomorrow." He paused. Worry hovered in the depths of her eyes. "I have faith that Stacy and Karl will be okay. They're very good agents. They know what they're doing. And don't worry. We'll be at the temporary safe house later today, and if all goes well you'll be in your new life tomorrow."

They lapsed into silence as the truck drove through the winter morning. The sun rose higher. They passed farms with rolling fields and empty roadside wooden fruit and vegetable stands that reminded him of those his mother had expected him and his brother, Amos, to help out with during the summer.

"Did you grow up in the city or the country?" Celeste asked after a pause so long he wondered if she'd fallen asleep.

He guessed she was trying to change the subject away from Dexter, the fallen marshal and what had happened at the farmhouse. He was thankful for it. He pressed his lips together for a long moment and debated how to answer. He didn't talk about his past for a very good reason. Most people knew nothing about the Amish, and the last thing he wanted was to listen to someone else's uninformed opinion about the world he'd grown up in or answer questions about why he'd left.

But maybe Celeste wasn't like most people. "The country."

"I always wanted to live in the country," she said. "I don't know why, but even though I'm a born-and-bred city girl, I always felt like something—God, maybe—was calling me to live in the country. When I was little, my parents used to rent this summer house, surrounded by nothing but trees and fields. I loved it. Then my parents both got cancer and we couldn't afford it anymore. There were a lot of medical bills. I always told myself that one day I'd save enough to buy my own place outside the city, but Dexter Thomes took all that." She looked up at him. "You know he stole all my money, too, after I turned him in? Took out multiple loans in my name, stole my identity and utterly destroyed my credit."

He didn't know what to say. "I'm sorry."

"At least I knew the risk I was taking. I chose to hunt him down and tell the feds what I found. I put myself in his crosshairs. All the other people who had their life savings, college funds and retirement nest eggs stolen didn't do anything. They just woke up one day to find their lives ruined. I just wish I'd found where he hid the money." Her hands clenched into tight fists on her lap. "Not to mention it looks like he's now using his stolen money to pay criminals to come after me."

Instinctively, his hand reached out and brushed her arm. Her muscles were so tense she might as well have been carved from stone. "Don't worry. I'll keep you safe no matter how many criminals he throws at you."

Something fierce flashed in the depths of her eyes. "And who's going to stop the next Rod Cormac from dying? Or get those people their money back?"

He didn't have an answer to that. Then again, he wasn't sure she was expecting one. After a while, he saw her eyes close and her lips move in silent prayer. He found prayer filing his own core, too.

God, I don't reckon You and I are on speaking terms. But, please be with Rod's family and friends right now. Comfort them in their sadness. Please, may no one else die because of Dexter and his crimes. And be there for Celeste, too. Help me keep her safe, protect her from anyone who would want to hurt her and make her dreams for the future still come true.

He'd seen the size of the new apartment he'd be moving her into tomorrow, and it was a long way away from a house in the country. He could still remember the day he'd stopped believing that God called anyone to anything. He'd been eight and had excitedly told his brother, Amos, who was then seventeen, that God had called him to be a cop. And Amos had told him that it wasn't God— it was his own stubborn willfulness, because he couldn't be both a cop and Amish.

He turned off the small rural highway onto a larger one. After a while, a large, expansive truck stop came into view. It was teeming with vehicles and several big chain restaurants. He pulled to a stop in a row in the back beside the big blue pickup. He cut the engine. "Now we grab our stuff, switch vehicles and get back on the road."

They hopped out of the black truck and into the blue one, after he'd done a complete sweep of the vehicle for tracking devices or anything so much as a speck of dust out of place. Thankfully, it was clean. A moment later they were weaving their way back through the crowded parking lot.

The smell of doughnuts and coffee wafted toward them. Normally he'd have taken her in to grab a quick bite before hitting the road again. It was easy to be anonymous in a crowd, and there was no way any criminal organization could have eyes on every single rest stop of the highway, even if they happened to either figure out or guess what direction they were headed. After all, WITSEC expected their marshals to spend just a couple of weeks with witnesses helping them integrate safely into a community and letting them know where to reach help before leaving them to live their new lives. Starting over safely was the goal—not spending the rest of their lives hiding behind a closed door.

Still, something about this particular case and this particular witness gave him pause. If Dexter Thomes had been able to find a WITSEC safe house, was it possible he'd be able to find her in Pittsburgh? It wasn't like hunkering down behind her computer screen and cutting off all contact with the outside world was going to be an option for Celeste. Hunter had been very clear the plan to ensure her safety involved keeping her off-line. Yes, they'd stop for food, and he'd use that opportunity to introduce her to the idea of watching her own back when he wasn't going to be there. His gut told him to find somewhere much smaller and more remote. Fortunately, he knew just the place.

Suddenly her fingers grabbed his arm and squeezed so tightly he almost winced.

"We need to go—now." She pointed with the other hand out the window at what looked like a remote-controlled helicopter hovering behind them. "Because I think we're being watched by that drone."

FIVE

The small skeletal machine hovered around the parking lot like a wasp looking for a place to land. She couldn't spot the person who was controlling it.

"It just looks like a toy." Jonathan shrugged.

The small device flew until it was almost parallel to the back window. It was only then she realized her fingers were still latched onto his bicep. She let go and pulled her hand back. "It might be a hobby drone, but that doesn't change the fact people can use them to take video and pictures."

"You think that toy helicopter is spying on us?" he asked. "Trust me, we weren't followed and nobody knows we're here." Well, when he said it like that she sounded ridiculous. But he didn't understand technology the way she did. "Don't worry, we'll be back on the highway in half a second, and if it follows us, I'll shoot it out of the sky."

Was he joking or trying to reassure her? Maybe both. His voice was so dry she couldn't tell. Moments later they were flying down the highway again. The drone didn't follow.

"Should we be worried that we haven't heard from anyone on your team yet?" Celeste asked.

"Not necessarily," he said. "We're talking about securing a sprawling location with multiple hostiles and possibly multiple casualties. It will take time. Hunter will want to get all her facts straight before she calls, including confirming Dexter Thomes is still safely tucked away behind bars. Not that I think it's remotely possible he could've broken out of prison without us knowing."

"So you're convinced we're dealing with a Doppelgänger-Dex?" she asked.

He chuckled. "Doppelgänger-Dex is what we're calling him now?"

"Unless you can think of a better name," she said. "Though maybe Doppel-Dex for short."

He laughed again. It was a comforting sound that rumbled from somewhere in the back of his throat. "Well, when the safe house is secured and someone on the team gets in touch, hopefully, they'll confirm that the real

Dexter is still in jail, the man you saw will have been apprehended and we'll know who he is."

"Hopefully." She leaned back against the seat. Her eyes closed. Jonathan Mast seemed to be a good man, and she had to admit there was something about him that made her feel safer than she'd ever imagined being able to feel under the circumstances. But between Doppel-Dex and the hobby drone, it seemed that the US marshal assigned to protect her probably thought she was crazy or at least seeing things.

The tablet full of data she'd gleaned from Dexter's website sat like a dead weight in her pocket. Were there answers on it? Something that would tell her where the stolen money had gone? If so, she had no idea when or how she'd ever be able to access it.

She hadn't been online or even been able to check her phone in almost three days and it irked her, like she'd lost a part of herself. She couldn't remember the last time she'd gone this long without scrolling through the news or logging into chat groups. She stared out at the endless countryside streaming past her window. All the plants and animals living on her virtual farm would probably be long dead before she could ever log back into it.

Yes, she'd chased down a criminal online and didn't regret it; however, she'd never imagined the cost would be getting cut off from technology and losing her ability to still do her job. And then there was her money being stolen, and the explosion in the apartment where she'd grown up with her parents, taking with it a lifetime of memories. She'd been left with nothing but borrowed clothes, a tablet full of data that she couldn't read and the protection of the man sitting beside her.

She cast a sideways glance at him. There was something about him that she just couldn't put a finger on. It was like some invisible piece of coding had created a glitch in the circuits in her brain. Or a kind of connection that drew her in and made her want to find out more, while also feeling the irksome urge to prove herself to him and to make sure he knew she wasn't just someone in need of rescuing. She couldn't begin to identify it or figure out the source code. Maybe it was because her entire life was in his hands. It couldn't just be how good-looking he was. She'd never thought herself shallow about people's looks. Although he was definitely handsome.

There was a strength to his body and form that made her think he should be tossing heavy bales of hay into a wagon or a barn, or herding cattle. Yet, whenever his hickory-brown eyes had fallen on her face, there was something protective and hardened in their depths that was all cop. Or if not a cop, then some other profession like a soldier, fire-fighter or paramedic, who ran into chaos and put their life at risk to rescue others. There was something sad about him, too, and a severity to the lines of his jaw that made her suspect he didn't smile enough and was in need of a good home-cooked meal.

His hair was properly black, not one of those shades of dark brown that people sometimes mistook it for. It curled slightly, down at the nape of his neck and on top, and she suspected that if he ever let it grow out it would turn into a full head of curls. His trim black beard swept down the strong lines of his jaw and under his chin, like an artist had defined them with charcoal. The eyes that scanned the snowy vista outside were dark and rich brown with black rings around the iris. If someone had ever asked her what she thought of brown, she'd have said she figured it was the least interesting color there was. But not this shade. Not his eyes. No, these eyes seemed to contain a depth that made her think of rich, dark earth.

His gaze snapped to her face as if realizing she was analyzing him. One eyebrow rose. "Everything all right?"

A flush of heat rose to her face. She'd always been awkward and never exactly good at small talk, which was probably why she'd never had so much as a successful date with a man, let alone an actual relationship.

"Sorry," she said. "I was just thinking that you know a lot about me and I know practically nothing about you."

He waited a very long moment, then asked, "What do you want to know?"

She bit her lip. What did she want to know?

"How long have you known you wanted to be in law enforcement?"

There was another even pause. A look moved across his gaze that was somehow deeper than sadness or even regret. Then when he spoke, she wasn't quite prepared for what came out of his mouth.

"Was I right in thinking you were praying back at the farmhouse?" he asked. She nodded. He turned away from her and stared straight ahead through the windshield, with one hand on the wheel and the other lying in the space between them. "Then I'm guessing you're familiar with the biblical stories about David and Jonathan. That's who I was named after, Prince Jonathan, son of King Saul. I couldn't get enough of those Old Testament battle stories as a child. There was nothing I wanted more than to be one of those heroes of old, the kind with a shield and sword, who worked together with others to save my country and the people in it from evil and tyranny."

A grin crossed his lips. It was unexpected, cute and infectious, and it somehow softened his face. She liked it. Then the smile faded again. He shifted his hand on the steering wheel.

"I didn't see my first cop until I was eight. My parents had me late in life and mother always had health and mobility issues, with her joints mostly. She had early onset of arthritis and some kind of nerve damage when she'd given birth to me. Her mind was really sharp, though, and she had the best sense of humor. Anyway, the summer when I was eight I was in town with my seventeen-year-old brother and my mom, and these tourists started bullying us. They yelled at us mostly, but also threw some trash and pushed my brother around a bit." He swallowed hard. "My mom fell."

She reached for his hand without even thinking and squeezed it. He squeezed her back for one long moment. Then he pulled his hand away.

"Then this man and woman in blue uniforms showed up and told them to leave us alone," he continued. "I knew then that's what I wanted to be. Then when I was twenty and studying criminology I realized that what I really wanted to be was a US marshal. Specifically I wanted to work in the protection side of law enforcement, as opposed to the detection side. I wanted to help catch fugitives. I wanted to transport prisoners. I wanted to protect endangered witnesses. I wanted to be out there, like Prince Jonathan from the Bible, with my shining shield and sword literally and physically protecting people every day. I wanted to protect people and keep them safe." A glimmer of a smile brushed his lips again. "Plus, I still really want to go out and fight the Philistines."

A laugh slipped from her lips, taking her by surprise. Her fingers rose to her lips as she felt her smile spread into her cheeks, and as his eyes turned to her face there was something new there, a glimmer of something that again she couldn't define. All she knew was that she'd never seen it before. For a long moment neither of them said anything.

"Are the stories of David and Jonathan still

your favorite part of the Bible?" she asked. "I've always loved the Psalms, Proverbs and Ecclesiastes."

"My father loves those, too. It's funny. You almost talk like him." Just like that the smile fell from his face and his hands snapped back to two and ten on the steering wheel. "I haven't picked up a Bible in years."

There was a tone to his voice that made her think of a book slamming shut or a door being locked. US Marshal Jonathan Mast was done sharing. Silence filled the car again. The longer it drew out, the colder and thinner the air felt and the more her chest ached.

Lord, I don't know why he opened up to me like that or what the pain is in his heart that pushed him away from You. But if there's anything I can do to help him, anything You want me to say, please let me know.

The truck slowed and it took her a moment to realize why. There was a horse-drawn buggy on the road ahead. A young man in a large brimmed hat held the reins. Jonathan gave him a wide berth, nodding to him as he passed.

"He's Amish, right?" Celeste asked.

Jonathan's gaze stayed fixed on the road ahead. "Yes, most of these farms are."

She glanced out the window, looking anew

at the large beautiful farms with barns and silos. "I haven't driven through the Amish countryside since I was a child. I always assumed my memories were larger than life. But it's every bit as beautiful as I remember."

"You should see it in late summertime," he said, "when the fields are full of flowers and the crops are almost ready to be harvested. There's no place more beautiful on earth."

She blinked. Had he really just said that? See, that was why he confused her. He could be so open and real one moment, and then shut off and closed the next.

Another buggy loomed ahead of them on her side of the truck. This one had a couple in the front, her large black bonnet tilted toward his bearded face as if whispering a secret in his ear. Six little heads, in hats and bonnets, bounced up and down in the back.

"It's funny," she said. "When we used to drive through the Amish country as a kid, all I wanted was to get out of the car and ride in a buggy. Now, I just wonder how they do it."

"You mean, how does a family take their kids out in a buggy in January?" he asked. "With a whole lot of blankets and warm clothing. What kid would want to be stuck sitting in the back of a car with seat belts on when they could be outside with the horses, and their cousins, brothers and sisters piled around them?"

She laughed. Yes, when he put it like that it definitely sounded better than being in a car. "No, I meant I can't imagine how people live entirely off the grid. No car, cell phone, internet or electricity."

"It's peaceful," he said. His voice dropped. "It's not right for everyone, but I have a feeling you're the kind of person who'd like it. Well, if you weren't a computer programmer."

She had the odd sense that he'd given her a bigger compliment than she'd realized. They lapsed back into silence after that, but somehow it was a more comfortable space than before. It reminded her of the kind of comforting quiet that surrounded her when she curled up with a good book or spent hours happily typing lines of code. Something about the faint glimmer of a smile on his face led her to believe he understood those kinds of silences, too. She wondered if he'd ever had anyone to share them with.

He turned onto a smaller rural road, passed a smattering of stores and then she saw the wooden sign for a diner ahead. He pulled in. It was a low and long building, with a spacious parking lot and a smattering of picnic tables. He parked in a wide open spot near the front of the lot.

"Hope you're hungry," he said. "The food here is great and the owners are really friendly."

"I'm guessing this place is part of some kind of witness protection network?" Celeste asked. "Cops on the door? Security measures?"

"Nope." He cut the engine.

"But Dexter Thomes has goons out to kill me! I can't just waltz into a diner and order scrambled eggs like a regular person."

"You can, and sooner or later, you're going to have to." He undid his seat belt and turned to face her on the seat. "Yes, we're taking a risk—a calculated one. Witness protection isn't about locking people away in a secure facility with guards on the door, and my job isn't just to watch your back 24/7. Not after the initial stage. Part of the purpose of witness protection is to equip you to live a fairly normal life and still keep yourself safe. There are people in witness protection who haven't actually seen an agent in months or even years, and just check in by phone regularly. After the initial transition and adjustment phase you're going to find you don't want to hide in your apartment with the door locked and the blinds down. Over time, you'll learn how to make friends, go shopping and live a fairly normal life. Starting with eggs."

Her head shook. "What do you mean some people spend months or years in witness protection without seeing a marshal? The trial is just a few months away. It's your job to protect us."

It's your job to protect me! I thought you'd be there for me as long as I was in danger!

"One thing I've learned about this work is that it's unpredictable," he said. "Last I heard the trial was scheduled for March. But trials get postponed for all sorts of reasons. I've seen trials get delayed for years because of appeals, charges get suddenly dropped over technicalities and people who've expected to be in witness protection for a few days end up in their new lives indefinitely. I won't always be able to be there every moment of every day to have your back, unfortunately. And you might have to hide from Dexter, and whoever he sends after you, for the rest of your life."

She looked away, but not before he could see the look of fear that washed across her face. Her gaze rose to the sky. Somehow he knew she was praying and couldn't shake the feeling he'd be the one breaking it to her that her prayers weren't going to be answered as she'd hoped. He'd hated telling her the truth about how long and lonely a life in witness protection could be.

She turned back. Her arms crossed and her chin rose. "Okay, so where do we start?"

Did she have any idea how extraordinary she was?

"Step one is only frequenting locations that you know are safe," he said. "Places with good lines of sight and good exits, that are run by honest people who aren't likely to be involved in anything illegal on the side or pry into your business. Once we get you settled into your new home, I can help you identify those. Step two is learning to fly under the radar."

He reached around into the back seat, opened his duffel bag and pulled out a baseball cap and shapeless black sweatshirt and handed them to her. "I'm hopeful we won't need to look at any drastic changes to your appearance. Still, the last thing you want to do is draw attention to yourself. Put these on."

He waited as she fished an elastic band out of her jeans and tied her hair back into a bun. Then she put on the sweatshirt and pulled the hat down over her head.

"I've never been into clothes or worn

makeup," she said. "I've always been pretty plain and nobody much cares what the person hiding on the other side of the computer screen looks like."

Plain? As in unattractive? Who was she kidding?

"Well, your new life isn't about hiding so much as being inconspicuous," he said, trying not to notice how beautifully the wisps of blond slipping out from under the hat framed her heart-shaped face. "It's about being the kind of person who doesn't get noticed. Which is hard for someone with looks like yours."

She blinked so hard her entire body sat back. Heat rose to the back of his neck. Had he really just said that out loud?

"What do you mean looks like mine?" she demanded. "You think I haven't heard enough men online and in person take potshots about my weight or my shape, or how thin my hair is, how funny-looking my nose is or how my eyes are too far apart?"

Wow, so she'd come across a lot of jerks in her life. She honestly didn't know that she was an attractive woman? How could anyone that exquisite go through life thinking they were funny-looking or plain?

"Well, despite what idiots might have told

you, you're kind of a head turner." His neck grew hotter. What was he saying? "Your hair is fine. Your face is fine. Everything all looks fine. Come on, let's go eat."

He pushed the door open and half stumbled out, like he'd spent too long on a boat and gotten sea legs. By the time he'd made it around to her side of the truck, she'd already hopped out and closed the door behind her. They walked over to the diner. His hand brushed her shoulder as they reached the door, and even through her jacket and sweatshirt he could tell she was shaking.

"Don't look so nervous," he said with a smile that he hoped was reassuring. "Compared to what you've been through in the past week, getting coffee and eggs should be a breeze."

He pushed the door and held it open for her, then followed her in and couldn't help but notice she was scanning the room the same way he would. He liked this diner. It was a long building and wider than someone would've expected from the outside, with two rows of tables. Chairs instead of booths made it easier to jump up at a second's notice, and along with the front door there was a large emergency exit at the side, not to mention a third exit through the kitchen. Two of the tables were occupied with elderly couples.

"Where do you want to sit?" he asked, tilting his head close to hers.

"I don't know," she said. "I'm just stuck thinking I'm going to have to walk into every building from now on wondering who's out to hurt me and how to escape."

"Trust me, it's not as bad as all that, and soon enough it'll be second nature. Now let's go eat."

He reached for her shoulder, but somehow as she stepped forward he found his hand sliding down to the small of her back, his fingers fitting so comfortably there it surprised him. He led her over to the table by the window and pulled a chair out for her, noticing the slight shake in her limbs as he did so. He understood why her legs were wobbly. Not as much why his were, too.

A middle-aged woman with spikey blue hair and a name tag reading Missy arrived almost immediately with menus, mugs and a pot of hot coffee. He thanked her and she left.

"It's a pretty simple menu," he said, sliding one of the two laminated sheets across the table to her. "I hope you like eggs."

A gentle smile lit her face.

"I like simple," she said. She looked down

at the menu. "There's nothing worse than those fancy coffee shops with hundreds of ways to order coffee. I always feel so awkward and uncomfortable and like I'm holding up the line."

"I like things simple, too," he said. There was a comfort in simplicity and that was part of what he liked about this place. There was one egg, or two or three, with bacon or sausage. There were pancakes and syrup. There was hot brewed coffee being poured into chunky and solid white mugs. Celeste chose two eggs with fruit. Jonathan went for three eggs with bacon. And they sat mostly in comfortable silence, exchanging simple furtive glances while they waited for the food. The late-morning sun sent dazzling rays bouncing off the blanket of crystal-white snow.

They finished their meal and sat for a long moment, just enjoying the coffee and the sunshine.

"How was it?" he asked.

"Amazing," she said. "I can't remember when I last had a meal that wasn't on my desk wedged beside my laptop."

The sound of children laughing dragged their attention to the door. A girl of about three charged into the room, followed by a young boy, a teenager and two tired but smiling parents. Missy met them at a table with menus and coloring pages. He guessed they were regulars. He watched as the mother pulled electronic game devices out of her bag and slid them in front of the younger two even before they'd settled into their chairs and wriggled out of their coats. Her own phone came out, too, and the father checked his before he examined the menu. The teen boy curled into a corner chair with headphones in and some kind of device Jonathan couldn't see hidden in his hands. He sighed.

"You don't like kids in restaurants?" Celeste asked.

"I love kids in restaurants," Jonathan said, turning back. "I love kids, period. I just don't like that they're so focused on their devices that they're totally ignoring each other. I don't doubt those parents love their kids. But I don't get the point of spending time with another human being only to ignore them."

"So, you're a 'no phones at the dinner table' kind of guy?" she asked.

He paused. How could he possibly explain to a computer programmer how he sometimes missed living in a home with no electricity?

"I'm a 'no electronic devices during family time' person," he said finally. "Anytime family members are gathered together, whether sitting in the living room, eating at the dinner table or curled up in bed at night, then the point should be to be together, not stare at flickering screens."

"Why Marshal Mast!" She tilted her head. "I didn't imagine you were old-fashioned."

"Well, if there's something old-fashioned about wanting to pay attention to the person you're with, then I don't much want to get with current fashion."

She laughed, then leaned forward. "Do you have any?"

"What, kids?" He blinked. Had she really just asked that? "No. No kids, no wife, no pets and no family. Family just isn't something that tends to happen easily when you're in a career like mine. I take it from your file you have no significant relationships? It's something we look into, because the last thing we need is some ex-boyfriend suddenly deciding to track you down."

"No, no relationships." A sad smile crossed her face. "I'm not for small talk, or dating, or any of that. The closest I've come is a very small handful of people I met online, who either turned creepy or disappeared suddenly without notice. Every date I've been on has been a disaster. It's hard to find someone looking for anything real, but so very easy to find men who want female attention. Dexter was one of those."

He leaned forward. "You had a relationship with Dexter?"

"No, he was fishing around online looking for female attention on some message boards I frequent. Any female attention. It wasn't personal. I didn't give him the time of day. But something about how he was talking about how brilliant Poindexter was got me thinking. It was an anomaly in the pattern. Men like that usually only talk about themselves."

His phone started to ring. He glanced at the screen and his heart leaped with joy.

"It's Karl!"

A smile broke across Celeste's face. Her gaze rose to the sky outside. "Thank You, God."

Thank You, indeed. He shot Karl a quick text telling him he'd call back in a second. Then he stood. "I'll go take it outside the back door while you go freshen up."

The emergency exit was right by the washrooms. Plus, the cold air might help snap his head back in the game. Something about being around Celeste made his head spin. She agreed. He left some money on the table to cover the bill, then walked to the back of the diner. He waited until she'd slipped into the ladies' room, then stepped out the back door and called Karl.

"Karl Adams."

"Hey, man, you have no idea how good it is to hear the sound of your voice!"

"About as good as I imagine it was to see your face in the hall." Karl's voice boomed down the line. "Hunter tells me you got Celeste out safely?"

"Absolutely. We just stopped for food, but you and I have a moment to talk without being overheard. What's the word?"

"The farmhouse is secured. Three hostiles were taken into custody. There were several minor injuries. Only one casualty."

"Rod Cormac," Jonathan supplied.

"Yeah." Karl let out a sigh. "Stacy is talking to his girlfriend and family now."

"He was a great marshal."

"He was the best."

A long pause spread down the phone as the two friends shared a silent and unspoken moment of grief. He was sure Karl was silently praying.

The easy way Karl talked about God jarred him somehow. He envied it. He missed the way his family had talked about God so easily around the farm, as if God really was, as his *mamm* put it, "the unseen guest at every meal." He admired the way Celeste kept turning to God for help and fully believed He had a plan for her life.

I miss talking to You, Gott. *But I don't even know how to come back to You.*

Karl went back to briefing him, this time in more detail and flavor. Jonathan held tight and listened. Only two hostiles in combat gear had breached the safe house. One, a career criminal who was already well-known to the feds, had been arrested, and one had escaped the net. Two more criminals, much younger and far less experienced, were picked up on the road shortly afterward. They'd been identified from the description Jonathan had given Hunter. Footage of Celeste had turned up on one of their phones. Karl had no way of knowing whether it was already uploaded to the dark web.

"I want to give you a heads-up," Karl said. "Chief Deputy Hunter has told Stacy and I to be prepared for a potentially quick assignment change. We were supposed to be doing a prisoner escort in Philadelphia tomorrow. But Hunter has said there's a possibility she might pull either Stacy or I to take over escorting Celeste. It's just a precaution. In case you've been identified. It happens to the best of us."

"I know," Jonathan said. He ran his hand over his beard. As much as something inside him hated the thought of Celeste being transferred to another marshal, he wasn't surprised.

"Is it true Celeste thought she saw Dexter Thomes in the safe house kitchen?" Karl asked.

"It's true that's what she thought she saw. She calls him Doppel-Dex. She also thought a remote-control helicopter was watching us when we stopped to switch trucks. I don't know what to think." He glanced back. Celeste was standing inside the diner with her back to him. He shifted his gaze. His heart stopped. She was scrolling through data on some kind of small electronic device. *What was she thinking?* "I gotta go. I'll call you back."

He hung up, slammed the phone into his pocket and yanked the door open. Celeste spin toward him. He snatched the device from her with one hand. The other hand grabbed hers and pulled her close enough that they could whisper. "What do you think you're doing?"

SIX

Conflicting emotions surged through him. Where had she gotten an electronic device? Yes, she'd told him she had a tablet with some of Dexter's data on it, but she'd also told him it was completely dead. How had she been foolish enough to use an electronic device when her life was in jeopardy and she was being hunted online by people who wanted to take her life? Why had he trusted her out of his sight for so long? What was it about her that had made him drop his guard like that and think he could trust her?

Yet, as he opened his mouth, it went dry, and all the questions that filled his mind died on his lips. Finding no words to say, he stood there, with his hand holding hers and her wide eyes looking up into his. Her lips were parted, half gasping and half panting in shock. Her body was so close anybody looking on would've been forgiven for thinking he'd spun her around to kiss her. He let go of her hand and looked up, breaking their gaze. No one else in the diner had seemed to notice their pirouette and he was thankful for that. He looked down at the device in his hand. Letters and numbers filled the screen. "What is this?"

"I told you, I had a tablet full of data that I downloaded from Dexter before he blew up my apartment." Her voice barely rose about whisper, but the frustration of her tone was unmistakable.

"You told me it was dead."

"I borrowed a charger from the mother of the device-addicted children," she said. "Don't worry. Like I told you, this device is perfectly safe. It can't connect to the internet. And I think I'm on to something with my hunch about number patterns. I think Dexter tried to track down someone specific. I think if I could just figure out who he was looking for, where he was looking for them, and why, I might have a lead on finding where he hid the money."

"How can you possibly know that no one is using this device to track you?"

"Because I know how electronic devices and the internet works."

"What if you're wrong?"

"I'm not!" Her voice rose for a moment. Then she seemed to catch herself and lowered her tone. "It's extremely unlikely. Extremely. But if there's even the possibility I could find that stolen money, it's a risk I'm willing to take."

"Well, I'm not, and it's my job to keep you safe."

The teenage boy at the table glanced their way, and even though Jonathan was confident he wasn't able to overhear them, he still held up a hand warning to Celeste to stop talking. Then Jonathan moved closer and dipped his head slightly. "Let's take this outside."

She pressed her lips together. He could tell there was more she wanted to say. Well, she'd have to wait. Clearly, something about her had distracted him so much he'd fallen off the ball. He turned the electronic device over in his hand. It was the size of the notebook that the waitress had taken his order on. He frowned and turned it around looking for a switch to turn it off. As if reading his mind, Celeste reached over, slid her finger along the side, her hand brushing against his for a fleeting moment as she pushed a button so tiny he couldn't even see it. The power light turned off.

"Thank you," he said. He slid it into his

inside jacket pocket. He reached down, unplugged the cord from the wall and rolled it between his fingers. His hand rested on Celeste's back just between the shoulder blades as they walked to the family, returned the charging cable with an exchange of polite smiles and then headed out the front door.

They'd gotten about five paces away from the door when Celeste stopped and turned toward him. Her arms crossed. "So why is it okay for you to take the risk of us stopping at a roadside diner, but it's not all right for me to take the risk of combing data on an off-line electronic device?"

Because it's my job to determine which risks to take. I'm the experienced US marshal entrusted with your safety, and you're the witness.

The answer snapped to the front of his tongue, but he held it back and instead took a deep breath. Celeste wasn't just any other witness. There was something special about her that he couldn't put into words.

"You're right," he said. "I took a risk in stopping here for food. Because despite what happened at the farmhouse, I'm still working on the presumption that my goal is to help you learn to live an independent life. There's a world of difference between walking into an out-of-the-way roadside diner and using an electronic device to track down a dark web hacker's stolen money. Especially since I'm guessing the feds already have the exact same data you have."

"They don't know Dexter like I do," Celeste said. "He wasn't even on their radar."

He scanned the parking lot. A small red car was parked near the front entrance with the hood up. It was only a few feet away from his truck. A couple seemed to be arguing over it. Looked like someone was having car trouble. He steered Celeste away from them and picked a safe middle ground where they couldn't be overheard by either the people taking care of the car or anyone coming out of the diner.

"But what if no one ever finds the money?" she pressed. "Dexter Thomes stole millions of dollars."

"From a bank," he said.

"No, from people who deposited money in the bank," she countered. "From parents, families, students, people living on their own and the elderly. He dipped his greedy hands into thousands of bank accounts."

She stepped toward him until they were almost toe-to-toe. He reached out, his gloved hand hovering just inches from her shoulder. Then he pulled back. Something weird seemed to happen whenever he even barely brushed against her. Instead, he crossed his arms across his chest. It was a stance and a gesture that usually intimated people and made them step back. Instead, she took another step forward, closing the remaining gap between them until she was almost stepping on his toes. "What's your point?"

"That I need to finish the job I started. I found the trail of bread crumbs. I didn't find the money. If I found the money and traced it back to him, they might not even need me to testify at trial. All this would be over. And all those people's lives would be changed."

"I get it," he said. "I really do. I just don't know what we can do about it."

Out of the corner of his eye, he was aware of movement behind them. It seemed the woman from the duo having car problems was coming toward them.

"Hey!" a female voice called. "You guys couldn't give us a jump, could you? I think the battery's dead."

He turned around, feeling Celeste one breath behind him. Normally the possibility that this obscure pair at a random country road diner would have anything to do with the witness he was protecting would've barely been a fleeting thought in his mind. It was just too unlikely. Yet, so much of what had happened since Celeste had been placed in his care made so little sense at all. The woman was younger than he'd realized at first glance. She was barely more than eighteen, with dark curly hair and baggy jacket. She looked more like the kind of person he'd expect to find trying to sell individual joints or small amounts of drugs outside a club than working for the world's top computer hacker. The scowling man standing beside the car looked at least ten or fifteen years older, with a large nose that had once been broken and scar on his neck from what Jonathan guessed was more likely a broken bottle than a knife. Whatever kind of relationship they were in, it probably wasn't a positive one.

"Sure thing." He smiled, putting a bit of extra drawl into his voice and dropping his law enforcement stance and posture in an instant. He glanced back at Celeste. "Honey, I'm just going to grab my jumper cables from my truck and give these two a boost. Then we're going to get back on the road."

While I make careful note of both these two, and then run them and their car through the system as soon as we hit the road.

The look of utter relief that flooded over

the young woman's face was so palpable it made his senses tense up even more. Okay, whoever she was she was definitely in trouble. She was also walking back to the car.

"Good news, Fisher!" she called. "This nice man is going to give us a boost!"

The man turned. A grimace crossed his face and his lips contorted into what Jonathan could tell was supposed to look like a grin. "Well, that's mighty kind of you."

Jonathan knew his own fake smile was a whole lot more realistic than this man's, but still he could feel his jaw tighten as his gaze swept over Fisher's form. Everything about him smelled trouble.

"Oh, no trouble at all," he said. "Just let me get my cables and—"

The soft yelp of fear and pain and danger that slipped from Celeste's lips was enough to make his own words stop in an instant and every nerve in his body leap to attention. He spun.

The young woman had pressed a handgun into Celeste's side.

SEVEN

It only took a fraction of a second's glance back to the sneering man to confirm what Jonathan's gut already knew. He'd pulled a gun, as well. *And I apparently totally underestimated the resources Dexter Thomes has and the lengths he will go to in order to hurt Celeste.* Two criminals, two guns, Celeste's life in the balance—and he was trapped in the middle. He let his eyes linger on Celeste's, hoping she was praying and that God was listening to her prayers. Then he glanced at the girl holding her at gunpoint. She was shaking like a rabbit. Fisher noticed it, too.

"Gina!" Fisher snapped. "Wake up! Put her in the car and don't let her move or I'll kill ya when we're done with her."

Gina hesitated. Her hand shook so hard he knew that if he spooked her she'd probably shoot Celeste by mistake. And Jonathan didn't doubt she was terrified enough of Fisher that she'd probably kill Celeste to save herself. Gina's fear shook something inside Jonathan. The criminals who'd breached the farmhouse had been well armed and focused. The kidnappers with the cell phone camera had been brash and arrogant. These two were a whole different breed of criminal. Edgy and not well armed, with more than a whiff of desperation. The worst part was that he had no idea how they'd found them. His truck was clean of tracking devices, and even if Celeste had been right about that toy helicopter taking pictures of his truck, how would it have possibly found them all the way out here?

"Gina!" Fisher barked. "Move! Now!"

How long would they have until someone in the diner noticed? How soon until someone came out the back door? How soon until someone new pulled in? What would happen if Gina and Fisher opened fire?

Oh Gott, I don't know what to pray. I don't know if You're listening. Just please, help. For so long I've felt like the fact I walked away from my family and Amish life meant I've lost any right to call out to You for help. But, please, don't punish Celeste for my mistakes. Save her, Lord. Help me save her.

Fisher was snarling now, barking orders at

Gina in a stream of swear words and threats. Jonathan blocked them out. Instead, his eyes focused on Celeste. She'd told him that Doppel-Dex had made it very clear he wanted her taken alive. He hoped that was true.

"Do what he says," Jonathan told Celeste. "Just go with her to the car. Trust me."

Because I'm going to take out Fisher, and then I'm going to come rescue you. But Gina needs to calm down first before she accidentally kills you, and I need you out of the line of fire.

He didn't know what he expected to see in her face in that moment. But through the fear that filled her eyes, he could see something deeper, something he hadn't been able to detect back in the darkened farmhouse safe house, but which now shone clear and vibrant in the light of day—determination. She was a fighter. She was determined to stay alive. And it strengthened his resolve not to let her down.

"Get down!" Fisher snapped. "Or I'll shoot!"

Sure thing. Jonathan crouched low, raised his hands and gritted his teeth. Through his peripheral vision he watched Gina and Celeste walk around to the side of the car.

"Hey, we don't want any trouble!" Jonathan

called. "Just tell me your price and maybe we can work something out."

"You want to know my price? Fifty thousand." Fisher aimed the gun between Jonathan's eyes. "I want all 50K and not a penny less."

50K? As in fifty thousand dollars? Gina opened the back door.

"Really? Wow, that's a lot of money," Jonathan yelled. *Come on, man, focus on me. Don't look at the women.* "Who's willing to pay that much for her? How do you expect to collect?"

Gina's hands shook as she nudged Celeste in the side with the gun. They climbed into the car.

"Shut up!" Fisher shouted. "Kneel down and put your hands on the top of your head!"

Jonathan stayed crouched and did none of the above.

"Look, let me give you a hot tip. Dexter Thomes, aka Poindexter, is still locked away behind bars. So whoever you think is going to pay you isn't him."

The man laughed. It wasn't pretty. "Do you think I'm an idiot?"

Yup. An evil and deadly one, who wasn't about to tell me anything I needed to know.

Gina climbed into the car and shut the door.

Jonathan charged and threw himself at Fisher. He stayed low, letting Fisher get a round off that flew over his right shoulder. Then, with one hand, he grabbed the gunman's wrist and yanked the gun up over his head. With the other he leveled a strong blow to Fisher's face. The gun flew from Fisher's grasp as the man crumpled against the hood, unconscious but breathing.

Jonathan glanced up at the faces of the two women sitting in the back seat of the car. Two pairs of wide eyes met his through the windshield, one terrified and one trusting.

He shoved Fisher's gun in his pocket and pulled his own trusty service weapon.

"Listen, Gina," he said, keeping his voice low like he was dealing with a spooked and frightened animal. "I don't want to kill you, and I don't think you want to kill her. I think you're just doing what you were told to do. Drop the weapon and get out of the car, nice and slow, and nobody needs to get hurt."

The young woman's head shook. "I can't… Fisher…"

"Fisher is unconscious, I have his gun and I can take you somewhere he'll never find you." Jonathan stepped closer and raised the weapon. He had a clear shot now, just past

Celeste's shoulder. One shot and Gina would be dead. But he really didn't want to take it.

Please let me help you.

A flurry of activity yanked his attention to the diner. The family was bursting through the door. The little girl screamed. The father shouted. Jonathan raised his badge and yelled.

"I'm a US marshal! Everyone get inside, lock the doors, stay away from the windows and call 9-1-1!"

A gun fired inside the car, sending glass flying as a bullet exploded through the windshield. Celeste tumbled backward out of the car and onto the ground, leaving Gina moaning and doubled over in the back seat. He blinked. Celeste looked up at him.

"She was going to shoot you," Celeste explained. "So when she turned and aimed at you, I grabbed the gun and kicked her with both feet."

The hat had fallen from her head. Her blond hair fell loose and wild around her shoulders. Gina's gun was clenched in her hand. Looking down at her, Jonathan felt like he'd lived a thousand lives in one instant. *You're the most incredible person I've ever met. If I feel all this for you after less than a day, how will I ever let you go when all this is done?* She handed him the gun. He took it with his left hand, then reached for her hand with his right and pulled her to his feet. Behind her, he could see Gina sobbing hysterically in the back seat of the car.

"Come on!" He squeezed her hand and felt it tighten in his. "We've got to run."

They ran for the truck. He threw the door open, and practically lifted her up into the passenger seat. He closed the door behind her the moment she was clear, then ran around to the other side, allowing himself one glance back. Fisher had roused and was groaning. Gina was crying so hard she her body shook. The diner's blinds had closed and the lights went off. He prayed for the safety of those inside.

"What were you thinking, fighting her for the gun?" he demanded. They peeled out of the parking lot. One hand was clamped on the steering wheel, the other dialed Chief Deputy Hunter. "Don't get me wrong. It was impressive. It was incredible. I can't tell if I should be in awe or infuriated. But you also should've trusted me to handle it. You could've gotten yourself killed."

"The gun wasn't pointed at me!" Celeste spluttered. "It was pointed at you. I'm not an idiot. I waited until she was distracted, I was out of the line of fire and then I fought her for it. It was smart."

"It was risky!" His head shook. The phone rang. He couldn't figure out if he wanted to yell at Celeste or kiss her right now. But neither was an option and neither urge made his job any easier. "Yeah, it was brave. You've got guts. I'll give you that. But if I die they'll just find another marshal to protect you. If you die, there'll be no one to testify against Dexter Thomes at his trial! Remember that!"

"Chief Deputy Louise Hunter." His boss's voice filled his earpiece.

"There's been an incident," Jonathan said. He filled her in quickly and gave her the location, a description of Fisher, Gina and the vehicle in rapid fire. "The diner seems to have gone on lockdown. Hopefully they've called 9-1-1."

"I'll make sure the 9-1-1 call went through and that authorities are on the way," Hunter said. "Where are you now?"

"We're back on the road and headed west. We're still en route to—"

The phone clicked. Celeste had hung up his phone.

"What are you doing?" he demanded, and the determination and fire in his face nearly shook her resolve.

Instead, her fingers tightened over the phone.

"What are you doing?" She threw his words back at him. "You wanted to get rid of my tablet, but you're still using a cell phone?"

"It's my work phone!" His voice rose.

"It's traceable and hackable!" Her voice rose to match it. "Do you think the fact I logged into the tablet is what made two random criminals show up at the diner? Well, I'm telling you it probably wasn't. Because it's not putting out a signal. Your phone is."

"You honestly think these criminals are sophisticated enough to hack a government-issued cell phone?"

"Yeah." Her chin rose. "I do!"

She could feel her feet digging into the floorboards beneath her feet. He was wrong, and she was right. She knew it. Problem was she had no idea how to convince him of that. He was the most stubborn man she'd ever met. And while she kind of admired his resolve and found it attractive, right now it was infuriating that he wasn't respecting her expertise.

"Look," she said. "I don't know how to convince you. I can't prove it to you without access to the right tools, and I might be wrong. Maybe both of our devices are clean and they found out we were there another way. But it's important you know that it's a possibility."

Jonathan's jaw set. His hands tightened on the steering wheel. He made a sharp turn to the left. The truck sped away from the highway and toward a strip of buildings.

"Let's set up a test of some sort," she said. "We put my tablet in one location and your cell phone in another. Then we wait and see if criminals show up at either place."

A run-of-the-mill truck stop was coming up quickly on their left.

"Can you wipe it?" he asked. "Quickly. Erase everything on it."

"Yeah, of course."

"Do it," he said. "Now."

He swiftly shifted into the left-hand lane. Her finger fumbled with the buttons. Was he really asking her to wipe a law enforcement cell phone clear? She took a deep breath and wiped it.

"Done," she said. "But a really tech-savvy person with the right skills and tools might be able to reconstruct some of it."

"Give it to me." He stuck his hand out and she dropped the phone into it. He pulled a hard left, crossing the highway and swerved into a truck stop. He rolled the window down, then as she watched, he smashed the cell phone hard against the side of the truck over and over again, until all that was left in his hand were cracked and mangled pieces. With the quick flick of his hand he tossed the pieces into a dumpster. Then he pulled back onto the highway. They sped in the opposite direction.

Her lips fell open. "I can't believe you did that."

"You made a good point," he said. "If you were wrong, I lost a cell phone. If you were right, my phone was putting us is danger. Now, can you give me your word that it is completely impossible we're being tracked through your tablet?"

No, she couldn't. Someone could have re-motely re-enabled the internet after she'd disabled it, or the device could've been infected with some kind of virus. But she was 99 percent certain and it was a risk she was willing to take. Did he have any idea how important the data on the tablet was? Or how impossible it would be for her to ever get her hands on it again? Frustrated tears pressed against the corners of her eyes. "No, I can't. It's very, very unlikely, but not impossible."

An access road lay ahead on the right. He slowed the truck and turned into it. Thick trees surrounded them on all sides. He pulled to a stop, turned and looked at her.

"Do you agree that our location is being tracked, somehow?" he asked. "We can agree on that, right? Because while there's no logical reason those criminals should've been able to find the location of the safe house, even if there was a leak within the US Marshals office—unlikely though that is—or they somehow hacked into somebody's emails, that still wouldn't explain how they found us at a random diner I told nobody we were stopping at."

"Agreed. Could they have tracked your truck?"

"Possibly." He stroked along the edges of his beard. "But that means they tracked both trucks, somehow, without knowing I was going to change vehicles, and decided to attack us in a public place instead of all the much more convenient and more remote places on the roads we've taken to set up an ambush. And between the clear blue sky and empty roads I definitely would've noticed if we were being physically followed."

She pressed her lips together. He was right.

"Please," she said. "Don't destroy this data. It's my only hope of ever finding where Dexter hid the stolen money. We can save it to a memory stick. Or even just print it! Paper is better than nothing. It doesn't have to be on an electronic device. I just don't want to lose it."

His eyes closed and for a long moment he almost wondered if he was praying. Then his dark eyes were on her face again. A smile crossed his lips that warmed every corner of her heart.

"I just remembered I have a memory stick that nobody's touched but me. Got it years ago and it's been on my key chain ever since. What if we transferred the data onto the memory stick and I promised to hold on to it until I find another option. Okay?"

She nodded. She didn't like it, but he'd smashed his phone because he'd trusted her. She could do the same and trust him. "Okay."

"Deal." He reached into his pocket, pulled out the tablet and gave it to her. Then he slowly worked a small, flat and bright yellow bobble off his key chain. "I got this years ago at a youth conference I went to as a teenager at a church that wasn't mine. The speaker talked about God having a plan for our lives and it was just so inspiring that I picked up a copy of the talk on the way out. I can guarantee that unless someone broke into my home and pilfered it from my bedside table while I was sleeping, or literally picked my pockets, stole my keys and slipped them back without my knowing, nobody has touched this but me. Is there any way people can trace the data itself?"

"Not if I save it as a plain text file." She plugged it into the side of the tablet, turned it on, converted the file to plain text and downloaded it to the memory stick. The whole thing took less than thirty seconds. Then she gave the tablet back to Jonathan. "Thank you."

"No problem."

He slid the memory stick back onto his key chain. Then he drove back and forth over the tablet until it was nothing but a collection of shards he then collected up and threw in a trash can. They kept driving. She leaned back in her seat and watched the memory stick swing as it dangled from the keys in the ignition.

Now what, Lord? I'm trying so hard to believe You have a purpose for my life. But I feel like I've just lost the last sliver of who I was.

"What do we do now?" she asked.

"I call my boss, fill her in on everything that's happened, make sure we're still on track as per our destination and get someone to meet us there with a new cell phone for me. I'm still not happy with the idea of you using an electronic device, not until we know more about what's going on. But I'll ask if somebody can bring us something we can use to print your data out on paper so at least you have something to go over it with. Oh, and also to bring you a box of pencils."

He cut her a sideways glance. A grin crossed his face and it was definitely growing on her. She felt a smile twitch at the corner of her lips. Had she ever smiled this much before? In school, she'd always been accused of being too serious and not knowing how to lighten up. Since then countless men in stores, coffee shops and the street had accused her of not smiling. Now somehow, in the middle of everything that had gone on, this one equally serious man was making her smile. It was an unfamiliar feeling. She liked it. "Don't forget a pencil sharpener."

He guffawed like a clap of thunder disappearing into the rain. "Deal."

The smile faded and a darker look moved through his features. He looked straight ahead again. "There's a town about thirty minutes east from here called Hope's Creek. It's pretty far off the beaten path, but it has public phone booths in the center of town. I can call Hunter's secure line from there."

"Public phones?" She couldn't remember the last time she'd seen a phone booth anywhere—at least one what was functional and not covered with graffiti. "What kind of small town still has public phone booths?"

"It's near a large sprawling Amish community." He still wasn't meeting her gaze.

"But the Amish don't believe in telephones! Just like they don't believe in electricity or cars."

A totally different laugh left his lips now. It was a bitter one that emanated from the back of his throat, and it was almost like he'd tried to bite it back and failed.

"You make it sound like they don't believe they exist," he said. "Of course they do. They just have a very different relationship with technology than the *Englisch*. That's the term they use for the outside world, and people like you and me. A lot of them hire cars, use electricity in their businesses or use public phones when they need to. They just don't believe in letting technology take over lives and ruin relationships. If you don't have a phone in the home, then you pay more attention to the people you're with. If you don't have electric lights you get better sleep at night and wake up ready to face the day. If you don't have a car…" His voice trailed off into a sigh. "If you don't have a car you never move too far away. Living by the *Ordnung*, which I guess you'd call the rules the Amish live by, is not about hiding from the world. It's about having everything in the correct balance, in relationship with others and *Gott*."

"Well, I didn't know that," she said. It was one of the longest monologues she'd heard come from his mouth. "But I like learning, and I've always wanted to know more about the Amish. The thing I'm going to miss most about the internet is the ability to find out about things I don't know much about."

He released a long breath.

"I'm sorry," he said. "That came out stronger than I intended. I just don't like anyone judging people by their appearances. And in my experience, too many people just see a beard or a bonnet, and don't even try to see the person underneath."

"Hey, I get it," she said. She reached across the center of the truck. Her hand brushed his sleeve and she felt the strength of his arm under her fingers. "It's okay. I'm a female computer programmer. I was the only woman in some of my university classes. I get horrible messages from strangers online when they realize I'm a woman. I get what it's like when people judge based on appearances."

He smiled. It was a good smile and a relieved one, like he was worried that he'd somehow offended her and was glad to know he hadn't. They lapsed into silence. The sun rose even higher. Bright blue filled the sky above them. Then she saw a buggy out her window. It was driven by an older man with a long white beard. Then there were more buggies with the young and old, men and women, families with kids, and groups she guessed were friends. She glanced at Jonathan. "I can see what you meant earlier. It does look like fun."

But his face was as serious as a man driving to his own funeral. She frowned as an uncomfortable thought crossed her mind, one that had been nagging at her for a while.

"Can I ask you a question?" she asked. "Why didn't you kill Gina? You had the shot. Instead, you showed mercy."

He ran his hand over the back of his head. "I didn't need to kill her."

"You didn't kill Fisher, either," she said. "Or Miller. Or Lee…"

"I haven't killed anyone," he said. "I'm not in the business of going around killing people I don't have to kill. Whether I'm escorting a prisoner who's trying to escape or part of a manhunt scouring the countryside for a criminal or putting my life on the line to protect a witness like you, if there's a way—any way—the criminal I'm up against can end up in court, facing justice instead of dying by my bullet, I will always choose justice and mercy."

"Have you ever taken a life?" she asked.

"No," he said. "A few times I've shot someone so severely I honestly believed the wound would be fatal. But each time, thankfully, they'd been saved by paramedics."

She paused, pondering her next question. Instead, to her surprise, his hand reached for hers and she felt the warmth of his fingers brush her skin.

"Trust me, Celeste," he added. "I believe in you. You stopped a criminal no one else could, and if anyone can find that missing money it's you. If I'm ever faced with a choice between pulling a trigger and letting somebody hurt you, I will save your life."

EIGHT

Not much had changed, Jonathan thought, as he slowly eased his truck toward Hope's Creek. It was a small town, with an official population of just a couple of thousand but many more living in the sprawling Amish farms spread out through the countryside, including his own family and people he'd grown up with. The ice-cream store was closed for the winter, but the faded sign was the same. The florist had a new name, but the hardware store looked exactly as he remembered it. Amish community, at least as he'd known it, had centered around family and friends. Even church had been held in the people's homes. Hope's Creek used to be his entire world. Yet, he couldn't say he had ever expected this to be his world forever. No, something inside him had always prompted and pushed him to go out into the world and make a difference.

As a child, he'd believed with his whole heart it was God. But his *bruder*, Amos, had told him in no uncertain terms that it couldn't be, and his *pa*'s quiet and stubbornly simple faith had made him feel impossible to talk to. Something defiant inside Jonathan had decided his only option was to leave. He'd been eighteen, mourning the loss of his mother and like a horse with blinders on. But now that he'd chased after that calling and become the man he'd thought he was supposed to be, where was he? The two parts of him were like oil and water, or two magnets repelling each other. Amos was right. He could never be both Amish and a cop. And now he was back, for the length of a single phone call, just a short buggy ride away from the only place he'd ever considered home.

He pulled into the center of town, near where the outdoor community phone boxes were or, at least, had been. A park bench sat where the community phone booth once had. But before he could worry about that a storefront caught his eye: Miriam's Second Hand Thrift Store. Handwritten signs in the window, in both English and Pennsylvania Dutch, told him they only took cash, all proceeds went to charity and that free clothes and food were available to those in need. More importantly, a large sign on the door mentioned there were community phones for free use within.

He pulled to a stop out front. Through the window he could see a striking woman in her late thirties in an Amish prayer *kapp*, dress and apron behind the counter. Beside her was a fresh-faced young man he guessed was probably no more than eighteen. He paused. Women running businesses in the Amish community were rare. At least in his experience. Was Miriam a young widow who'd started her own business after her husband's death? Was it a family-run business?

"I'm going to go in there and use the phone," he said.

"Can I come, too?" she asked.

He paused. His eyes scanned the street. Yes, she'd probably be safer in the store than she would be sitting out in the truck. "Sure, but hide your hair under the hat and stay close."

He walked around to her side of the truck, opened the door and reached for her hand. She took it, hopped out of the truck and gave him a weak but honest smile. They started across the frozen ground toward the thrift store and it wasn't until they pushed through the door that he realized he was still holding her hand.

The store was brightly lit and larger than he'd expected from the outside, with neatly arranged racks of *Englisch* clothes, displays with beautiful quilts and blankets, beautiful displays of secondhand furniture, and tables selling Amish preserves, jams, jellies and breads. A large display on one wall, with a world map covered in pins, outlined the charitable work in both the United States and overseas that proceeds went to funding. A sign above it in English and Pennsylvania Dutch read Be a Light in the World. His heart warmed.

Celeste read a large sign surrounded by smiling daisies and sitting on the front counter: Questions about Amish life? Please Ask. She pointed to it. "I guess that's one way to deal with ignorant people like me."

"I never said you were ignorant." And never would.

"Maybe not, but I know I have a lot to learn."

A light shone in Celeste's eyes as she scanned the store, full of curiosity and inquisitiveness, and it almost reminded him of the spark he'd seen in her eyes when she'd talked about the data.

"Can I help you?" the young Amish man called.

He stepped out from around the corner and crossed the floor toward them. The teenager's voice was polite, but his blue eyes were guarded in a way that made Jonathan remember how he and his brother had been harassed by tourists when they were younger. His name tag read Mark. A second slightly larger badge read Feel Free to Ask Me about Amish life, and Jonathan felt the odd impulse to clap Mark on the shoulder and tell him in Pennsylvanian Dutch that he knew firsthand that took courage.

Instead, all Jonathan said was, "We're looking for a phone."

Mark pointed to two stalls near the back, each with a small chair. "This way."

"Danke." Jonathan nodded and Mark withdrew.

Jonathan scanned the space between the phones and the front door. The lines of sight were clear. There was only a smattering of other customers in the store. He'd be able to get from the phone to anywhere on the floor in about two seconds flat. Besides, he really didn't want her listening in on his next conversation with Chief Deputy Hunter. Karl's warning that he and Stacy had been told to be ready for a potential assignment transfer irked him at the back of his mind. There'd been multiple attempts on Celeste's life. Fisher and Gina had definitely seen his face. A transfer was the logical next step.

But somehow I'm not quite ready to say goodbye.

He glanced at Celeste. "I'm going to need a moment of privacy. Are you going to be okay if I leave you? Don't go out of the store. Stay within eyesight of the phone booth. Browse and if you find any clothes you want or things you'll need, feel free to fill a basket or two. I think I even saw some luggage and toiletries, and I'm sure you'd appreciate getting some new stuff."

Not to mention he'd like to give this business a large donation when he left.

His hand slipped from hers, but she squeezed his fingertips tightly before they could fully let go. "Thank you."

He pulled away and then watched as she walked over to the woman with auburn hair behind the counter. A wide and welcoming smile filled her face as she came around the counter to greet Celeste, and Mark stepped behind the till to take her place. Sure enough, the woman's name tag read Miriam.

He left Celeste in animated conversation with the other woman, went into the phone booth and dialed his boss's number. She answered immediately.

"This line isn't secure." Had the last line been?

"Understood."

He briefed her quickly, filling her in on how they'd destroyed their electronics because Celeste had been concerned they could be hacked. It was odd, as he said it, how he'd trusted her implicitly, like she wasn't the person she was protecting but a partner or a member of the team.

He watched as she and Miriam were joined by a younger Amish woman he guessed was Mark's sister and a year or two older. She led Celeste through the store, their heads bent together like old friends. He couldn't look away from the smile that brushed Celeste's lips.

She's extraordinary, God. She's like nobody else I've ever met. She's this exquisite combination of beauty, brains and heart that just tumbled into my life, for a short period of time, and knowing me I should be irritated or annoyed at knowing it can't last. But in-

stead I'm just too amazed that she exists at all and happy that I ever got to meet her. So please, I'm asking You, watch over her, protect her, guide her, keep her safe and make all her dreams come true.

"Under the circumstances we think the best course of action is a transfer of marshals," Hunter said. "I'd like you to head to south. P. will meet you and take over your current assignment. You'll be temporarily assigned to work with A. for the time being."

In other words, he was to head to the southern Pennsylvania safe house, he'd be reassigned to work with Karl Adams and Celeste would be transferred into Stacy Preston's care.

He gritted his teeth. He wasn't surprised. He'd seen this coming. The only thing that mattered was Celeste's safety. Yet, somehow, the words still landed like a little flurry of punches knocking the air from his lungs.

"Understood." He knew the place. They'd be there in half an hour. Then Celeste would disappear from his life, he'd be on to a new assignment and he'd never even know for certain where she'd gone or how to ever contact her again.

He ended the call, but instead of crossing

the floor to find Celeste, he found his footsteps taking him to a secluded part at the back of the store that he guessed was the processing center for donated goods. Twin boys, with auburn curls like Miriam's were playing on a carpet with a pile of colored blocks. He guessed they were about four or five.

A stack of Bibles and prayer books, in English and Pennsylvania Dutch, sat on a wide wooden shelf next to a sign reading Free! Take One! Something inside him itched to reach for one. Instead, he leaned his back against the wall and pressed his hands over his eyes.

I feel so lost. I don't even know why I keep crying out to You when I'm sure You've given up on listening to me. But something about Celeste keeps pushing me here, to this point. So, I'll ask, what was the point of all this, Gott? Celeste is so certain that You have a purpose for people's lives? But what could the purpose possibly be to bring her into my life only to disappear again?

He took a deep breath and wiped his eyes. He'd barely taken a step when he felt a hand, heavy and strong, land on his shoulder. Somehow he knew who it belonged to even before he turned to face to see the cinnamon-brown beard and dark piercing eyes awash with confusion, sorrow and anger.

Amos.

"Pa!" the boys cried, leaping to their feet and running toward Jonathan's older brother.

"Bruder." Amos shook his head. "What are you doing here?"

"It's simply beautiful," Celeste murmured, letting her fingers brush over the intricate quilt patterns. The stitches were so neat, even and precise. It was hard to believe they'd been done by the young woman standing beside her.

"Do you sew?" Rosie asked. She had said she was eighteen, Mark's older sister and Miriam's daughter. A strawberry blond wisp of hair slipped out from under her white cap.

"No," Celeste said. "I always wanted to learn, but I never had the opportunity. I did teach myself to knit off an internet tutorial once. I made myself a sweater." She shook her head. "I'm sorry. You probably don't know what the internet is."

Rosie laughed. It was a soft, kind and inclusive laugh that seemed to pull Celeste in instead of making her feel like she was getting mocked. "Yes, I know what the internet is. We just don't use it. When Mamm doesn't need me in the store, I teach school."

"You're a teacher?" Celeste felt her eyebrows rise.

"I am," Rosie said. "My mother was a teacher before she married my *pa*. When he died, she moved here with my *bruder* and I, and started this store. Then she found love again and now the family is larger."

There was a twinkle in her eye that told Celeste there was a story there. She glanced at Miriam, who now crouched down, arms wide, to welcome two small boys charging through from the back of the store. She couldn't believe the courage of a woman who had started her own charity, helping others, as a widow in a new community, with two small children. "God always has a plan."

"Yah!" A wider smile burst across Rosie's face. *"Gott* is always *gut!"*

"I believe that, too," Celeste said softly. Or at least she always had. Unexpected tears rushed to her eyes and she wasn't quite sure why. She blinked them back. "I'm sorry, I'm afraid I don't know much about Amish life, but I really enjoy your patience in answering my questions. I feel like I've asked so many so far."

"It's okay," Rosie called. "As Grossdaadi says, the purpose of a light is to shine."

Grossdaadi. Would that be grandfather, Celeste guessed? She'd been able to piece together the little bits of Pennsylvania Dutch that Rosie slipped into conversation, like *yah* for yes, *Gott* for God, *mamm* for mother and *gut* for good.

"I was wondering how you sew your dresses," Celeste admitted. "The folds are so neat and precise, but I don't see any zippers or buttons."

"We use pins," Rosie said. "Would you like me to show you?"

"Please."

A shadow moved past the door. She looked up. A man was standing outside by the truck. He was heavyset, with broad shoulders, tinted glasses and an unkempt shaggy beard.

And my eyes are telling me it's Dexter Thomes, even though my brain is telling me that it can't be.

He was here. Somehow, he'd found her. But how? They'd gotten rid of the cell phone and the tablet. They'd changed trucks. But here he was, scanning the streets of the small town like he was looking for something, and she knew without a shadow of a doubt he was looking for her. Through the gap in his open jacket she could see the handgun concealed just inside his jacket.

"Excuse me," she said. She turned and started through the store toward the bank of phones. Her heart stopped. The phone sat there in the cradle and she couldn't see Jonathan anywhere. Her heart pounded hard in her chest.

Help me, Lord. Where is he? Where has he gone?

She glanced back to the street. The doppelgänger Dexter was looking in the window. She quickly shielded her face and turned away.

"Everything all right?" Rosie asked.

Celeste's head shook. "No, it's not. I came in here with someone. A man. And now I can't see him anywhere."

She scanned the store. Panic, swift and sudden, rose upside her chest like a wave. Where was he? He wouldn't just have disappeared or left the store without telling her.

Help me, Lord! I don't know what happened to Jonathan!

The front door jangled. She looked up and her heart stopped as Doppel-Dex walked through the door. She dropped to the floor, behind the rack of dresses, and hid, peering through the fabric at the same hulking form she'd seen back in the farmhouse kitchen. Whoever he was, he looked enough like Dexter Thomes to fool the average person. Especially if they'd only seen him through a video screen.

"I'm looking for this woman!" He slapped a cell phone down on the desk in front of Mark and Miriam with the screen up. "Her name is Celeste Alexander, and I'm offering a lot of money for anyone who tells me where she is. You people understand money? You tell me if you see her. I will give you money."

Miriam's eyes dropped to the picture on the screen. Her lips moved in what Celeste guessed was silent prayer. But Mark's young eyes seemed to cut straight across the room in her direction as he called out something in Pennsylvania Dutch that she didn't understand. *Help me, Lord!* A hand brushed her sleeve. She clamped her hand over her lips to keep from screaming. Then she felt the rustle of fabric and realized Rosie had dropped down and crept over beside her. The younger woman's eyes met hers, wide and filled with a fear that mirrored her own. "Are you in trouble? Do you need help?"

Celeste nodded. "Yes. Please hide me."

NINE

Jonathan stood in the back of the shop and just listened as Amos told him how much his absence had hurt him and their *pa*, and how his father's health had declined in his absence. How Amos's heart had been swallowed up in anger for a long time until a beautiful widow named Miriam, who was a couple of years older than he was, had moved to town with her two young children. She had challenged him to open up his heart to God and the world again. What was there to say? He was guilty of everything Amos was accusing him of. And his brother wasn't even yelling. Instead, his older brother's voice was every bit as level and calm as their *mamm*'s used to be. There was a softness to his brother's eyes, too, and a slight graying of his hair at the temples. He was a father now, a husband, and he'd taken care of everything on his own after Jonathan had left.

How will he ever forgive me?

"Talk to me, bruder," Amos said, his arms crossed. "You disappear for years and then I see you standing here in my family shop dressed like an *Englischer*?"

Where did he start? There was so much he wanted to say. So much he wanted to ask. He wanted to tell Amos he wasn't sorry he'd become a marshal, but he was incredibly sorry for how he'd left, and he wished there'd been a way he could go back in time and do it all better. He wanted to ask the names of his sons and what it was like to become a father. He wanted to explain just how strongly he'd felt called to protect others and how deeply it had hurt when he felt Amos had rejected him.

But all the words fell silent on his lips as he stood face-to-face with the brother he'd fought with, lost, missed and regretted hurting.

"I was wrong," Jonathan said. "Forgive me."

Before Amos could respond, voices rose behind them. Up to this point he'd been able to tune out the sounds of conversation coming from the store behind him. But now someone was yelling, his voice bellowing and echoing as swear words poured from his lips. Amos's head turned sharply at the sound of raised voices in the store. Jonathan followed his gaze. A large bearded man with long shaggy hair and tinted glasses was standing at the front desk, pointing his finger at Miriam and Mark. And as Jonathan watched, all the doubt he'd been feeling disappeared from his mind in an instant. While his brain knew this man must be imitation, he looked exactly like Dexter Thomes. Celeste had been right.

Celeste!

Desperately he scanned the store for her. Where was she? Where had she gone? *Help me find her, Lord!* He'd lost sight of her for only moments and now she was gone. Amos turned to go, but Jonathan clasped a hand on his shoulder.

"I'm sorry," he said quickly. "You deserve an explanation and my time. But it has to wait. I am a US marshal with witness protection. I am here guarding a woman whose life is in danger. That man wants to hurt her. We came in here together, and she is now missing."

The hostility faded in an instant from Amos's face. No matter how he felt about Jonathan and no matter how deep the rift they needed to mend, he understood.

"Where was she?" Amos asked.

Relief filled Jonathan's core. Amos was a better brother than he deserved right now.

"She was there," he pointed, "talking to the young Amish woman."

"Miriam's daughter, Rosie." Worry floated deep in Amos's eyes. Then he glanced at Jonathan. "This man is looking for you, too, yes? Stay here."

Amos strode across the store floor, his shoulders back and his head held high, radiating the strength and confidence that Jonathan as a child had both admired and been intimidated by. Jonathan watched as he exchanged a few brief words with Doppel-Dex, then the man stormed outside. Amos locked the front door behind him and switched the sign in the window to Closed. Mark moved immediately to shut the blinds. As the young man did so, Amos waved Jonathan to join them. Jonathan glanced out the front window through the gap in the closing blinds. Doppel-Dex was standing on the sidewalk outside the store confronting people with Celeste's picture.

"What did you tell him?" Jonathan asked.

"The truth." Amos's strong arms crossed his broad chest. "That I have not seen the woman he is looking for and we are closing for a family emergency." Then he turned to

Miriam, and an unexpected sweetness filled his gaze. "Miri, this is my brother, Jonathan, the *Englischer* US marshal."

Jonathan turned to Miriam and nodded. "It is very wonderful to meet you. I'm sorry the circumstances are not better. I'm looking for the woman I came in the store with. Have you seen her?"

She nodded and pulled the two small boys closer to her.

"It is a joy to meet you," she said. "You have already met Mark. These are our other boys, David and Samuel." Her eyes darted to the sidewalk, then back to Jonathan. "Come."

She led them through the store to the display table and pulled up the cloth. Two women in Amish clothing hid under the table, their white starched prayer caps close together as if in prayer.

"You can come out," Miriam said softly. "It's safe for now. He's gone. But stay low."

The young woman Amos had called Rosie slipped out first. But it was the second woman who seemed to catch his very breath in her hand and hold it. A long gray cape was draped around her shoulders, a white cap sat pinned over her blond hair. Green eyes met his.

Celeste! Thank You, Gott!

He crouched down, reached for her hands and helped her up. "Are you all right? What happened?"

"Doppel-Dex." The name slipped from her lips in a gasp of fear. Her hand tightened in his. "I saw him outside. Then he walked through the doors and Rosie hid me."

"And the quick change into Amish clothing?" he asked.

"That was Mark's idea," she said. "Mark said something in Pennsylvania Dutch about how my clothes looked exactly like the picture. Dexter didn't understand him, but Rosie did. She grabbed clothes and helped me get changed as best as we could in hiding."

He glanced from his brother, Amos, to the family that he didn't know he had. Gratitude filled his heart.

"You saved her," he said. "Thank you."

Celeste turned to Jonathan. "We need to get out of here and fast. These lovely people have done more than enough, and I don't want them in danger."

She was right. True, Doppel-Dex was gone and Amos had locked the door behind him, but he was still between them and the truck and there was no telling what he'd do. He turned to his brother. Conflicted feelings churned in Amos's eyes, as if his heart was being overwhelmed by more emotions than he knew how to process. Miriam's hand brushed her husband's arm. His touched her shoulder protectively. Her hands slid gently to her stomach.

"This woman is in trouble," she said gently. "We must help her escape."

Amos reached for his wife's hands, enveloping them in his own.

"My responsibility is to protect you," Amos told his wife in Pennsylvania Dutch, his voice husky in a way Jonathan had never heard before.

"And you always do," his wife replied. "Now God is calling us to help them."

As Jonathan watched, he saw an understanding dawn in his eyes that he knew an hour-long conversation of his most persuasive arguments could never have accomplished.

"Jonathan," Celeste said softly. "We can't let them help us."

"Trust me," he whispered, knowing those words were far too little and yet all he could say. "Please."

He could tell by the fire that flashed in her eyes that trusting him was the last thing she wanted to do right now, and while normally he admired her tenacity, right now her patience was what he needed most of all. How would he ever explain to her what was happening? Not just that as soon as they were safe she was going to be transferred to Stacy's protection. But that he had an Amish family he hadn't told her about and hadn't seen in almost a decade due to his own stubborn heart? He'd never opened up about his home life or past to anyone, and now he needed to in order to keep her alive.

Amos's hand landed protectively on Jonathan's shoulder. "Tell me what you need."

He turned to face his brother. His eyes were serious, kind and strong.

"I need a way out of this building and this town," he said, "where Celeste can't be spotted or traced. I need to get to a new vehicle that hasn't been seen by the criminals who are after her and a way to get my truck out of town."

His brother ran a hand over his long beard.

"Go with Mark," Amos said. "He will find you clothes to change into so that they do not recognize you. There is also a basket of food in the back room I packed for lunch that you can take. You need to make a phone call and tell your people about the criminal here, *yah*?"

"*Yah*." Jonathan nodded. Doppel-Dex was

still pacing outside, showing people Celeste's picture. They had to hurry.

"Okay," Amos said. "I will take Celeste with me and the family now to the buggy. The *Englischer* will not look closely at one Amish woman among many. Once I have left my family at a friend's house where I know they will be safe, I will come back with the buggy and meet you and Mark outside of town. I will then drive you to the home of an *Englisch* mechanic we do business with who sells old vehicles. He will have something that you can use to continue on your journey."

There was a finality to the way he said the word "journey." It implied he knew his brother was passing through, and Jonathan couldn't say he was wrong. He swallowed hard.

"Mark has many good friends at the *Englisch* church," Amos added. Something flickered in his eyes, making Jonathan suspect his brother was conflicted about how close Mark was to the *Englisch*. He wondered if his father was, too. "I am sure one of them can take your truck when the criminal has gone and leave it parked somewhere out of town."

His brother had always warned him of the evils of the outside world, and here Jonathan had come home, bringing that evil with him. He glanced from his brother's face to the members of his family searching for words to say. Then he turned to Celeste and took both of her hands in his as a thousand unspoken words bubbled up inside him. Instead, he said, "Amos is my brother. These people are my family. Go with them. They'll keep you safe."

He turned to go, trying to pull his hands from her grasp. Instead, she held on tight.

"You have to tell me something more than that."

"I know," he said. "But it's going to have to wait."

He broke her gaze. There was a very real possibility that Celeste might never forgive him for not telling her that he was Amish, he thought as he followed Mark quickly through the store and into the back room. After all, in the conversations they'd had about the Amish, he'd never once told her that he'd grown up Amish or they were in his own hometown. And he knew, if he was honest, that telling himself that it was just because he was the US marshal assigned to protect her wasn't good enough. As it was, leaving Celeste's side had felt not unlike tearing the thin roots of something just beginning the sprout out of the soil.

Mark led him through back rooms, full of

donated clothes to be sorted, used furniture and discarded electronics. The sheer number of old televisions and computers was staggering.

"Nobody will take them," Mark said, as if clocking Jonathan's gaze. "They never do. Mamm has gotten people to come in and fix them, but everybody wants something new."

Mark pulled a white shirt out of a bag and fished a pair of suspenders out of another one. Then he handed him a coat and hat off a set of hooks by the door.

"Thank you," Jonathan said, quickly trading his clothes for the ones Mark offered.

"No problem." Mark shifted his weight from one foot to another like he wanted to ask a question but didn't know how.

Jonathan slipped his apartment key and the memory stick of data off his key chain, slid them into his pocket and handed Mark the truck keys. "You'll find it out front. Blue Ford. Dented back fender. Hershey plates."

Mark nodded and took the keys. Jonathan watched as deep worry and pain filled the young man's eyes. He suspected the person Mark was worried for wasn't himself.

"You look like you want to say something," Jonathan said.

"Your brother is a very good man," Mark

said. "So is your father. They took very good care of us and welcomed us into their family."

A family that Jonathan had abandoned.

"And I hurt them very much," Jonathan supplied. Mark nodded. "I was angry about my mother's death. Amos and I were fighting about everything. He wanted me to step up and get baptized. I couldn't talk to my father. The way he talked about God made no sense to me. I thought God wanted me to be a cop. Maybe He did. But I went about it the wrong way."

"Amos will forgive you and help you," Mark said. He shifted his weight from one foot to another as if weighing his words. "Because he is a good man. When he tells your father, Grossdaadi Eli will forgive you for being so close to the farm and not visiting."

His words cut Jonathan deeper than Mark would ever know.

"Do you think that they are wrong to forgive me?" he asked.

"No, I am worried you will hurt them even more," Mark said. "Especially Grossdaadi Eli. He is growing old. When Mamm and Amos married, he was slow. Now he is much slower. You have to sit, then wait and wait for him to say anything. Then when he does talk it's all from the Bible and you have to guess what he means. It's like he knows the scripture so well that whenever his brain is slipping and can't find the words he wants, *Gott*'s words are what his mind reaches for."

Something caught in Jonathan's throat. Was his father slipping into early onset Alzheimer's or dementia? Or just slowing with age? His father had always been a very quiet man and slow to speak. He'd gotten married later in life, had Jonathan when he was nearing forty and was now in his midsixties.

"How do they feel about you having friends at the *Englisch* church?" Jonathan asked. He didn't know how his father would have felt with him going to an *Englisch* church when he was Mark's age, but he would've expected Amos to have a problem with it. Maybe Amos had changed or Jonathan had been wrong about him. Or both.

"They know that I want to follow *Gott*, but don't know yet if I want to be baptized," Mark said. "They think I should. But I feel like *Gott* wants me to wait."

"I'm sorry," Jonathan said. "I know how hard that can be."

"Do you?" Mark asked and Jonathan could sense genuine questioning in his voice. "Every time I try to talk to them about the *Englisch* church and baptism, I think they're afraid of losing me like they lost you. And I could never imagine leaving my family."

These people were Jonathan's family? The thought rattled in her mind as she quickly followed Amos out of the store and onto the street the moment he gave the all clear that Doppel-Dex had gone. Rosie flanked her on one side and Miriam on the other, holding each of the boys' hands in one of hers. Conversations she'd had with him in the diner and on the road flickered through her mind. He'd had so many opportunities to tell her about his family and hadn't. Maybe because despite whatever warm feelings he'd kindled inside her, they weren't actually friends or had any relationship besides the fact he'd been assigned to protect her. She'd been foolish to even imagine for one fleeting second it had been any other way.

She scanned the street. The blue truck was still there where they'd left it. Doppel-Dex was nowhere to be seen.

"Keep your head down," Rosie said softly. "Amish women don't greet strangers on the street."

She followed them along the street and then behind the store. There stood a magnificent dappled horse and simple black buggy sitting outside under an overhang.

"Is the horse out here all day?" Celeste asked.

"No," Amos said. "Thankfully, I had just come to the store to bring my family lunch. We always pause to have a meal together."

She watched as he helped the boys scramble into the back of the buggy, followed by Rosie.

Miriam smiled kindly at Celeste. "Now, watch what I do and I'll show you how to climb up."

"Hey! You!" A voice, loud and vulgar, seemed to shake the quiet laneway. Her heart stopped. Doppel-Dexter charged down the quiet road toward them. "Stop!"

Fear poured over Celeste like cold water.

Help me, Lord. Protect me. Protect these kind people who've helped me.

"Go," Amos said quietly. "Get in the buggy."

But she couldn't. Instead, her feet seemed rooted in place, just like they had back in the farmhouse tunnel. Jonathan had called it "shock," but it felt more like she'd suddenly turned to ice, both shaking and immobile at once.

Miriam climbed into the buggy and settled on the seat. Without a word, she reached down for Celeste's hand.

"I said stop!" Doppel-Dex raised his hand, brandishing a handgun. He pointed it at them like he was punctuating the sky. "Somebody said they thought they saw the girl I'm looking for go into your store."

Amos turned to face him. She realized Jonathan's brother was positioning himself between her and the man who was willing to risk so much to get his hands on her.

"My store is now closed," Amos said. "If there was a girl in there, she is not there now."

Doppel-Dex stopped just feet away from them. He was so close that Celeste could smell the stench of cigars on his clothes. Who was this man? Why was he hunting her? Was he using the money Dexter had stolen to hunt her? Why did he look almost exactly like the criminal who was now in jail waiting for the day she would testify against him and put him away for good?

And, above all, one question burned larger and larger than the rest—how had he found her?

She kept her eyes on the ground, fighting the temptation to look up in his face and search his eyes for answers.

"You have a very nice family here," Doppel-Dex snarled. "You really want to risk something bad happening to them by protecting some woman you don't even know?"

Amos didn't answer. Instead, Jonathan's brother just stood there, a pillar of silent strength and resolve in the face of the criminal's taunts.

Doppel-Dex swore at him. Ugly words and threats poured from his lips, and as they stood there silently in the face of his vulgar onslaught she suddenly remembered the story Jonathan had told her about the bullies they'd faced when they were children. For a second, standing there, it was like her heart was split in two thinking about the two very different brothers they'd been. One brave enough to stand strong and resolved in the face of bullying. One equally brave feeling called to fight back.

Lord, please, save and protect this family! I don't know what the hurt or pain was that drove Jonathan and his brother apart. But, please, keep them safe. Heal their brokenness and pain. Don't let them get hurt because of me.

"How about you, girlie?" Doppel-Dex focused his attention on her. He held his cell phone up. "You seen this woman?"

Her chest tightened. She locked her eyes on the ground and tried to breathe.

Please protect me, Lord.

Doppel-Dex walked up to her. Beside her, she could feel Jonathan's older brother step protectively toward her.

"Hey! Girl!" His voice rose. "You speak English? You know I'm talking to you, right? Do you have a tongue in your head?"

Her body shook. The prejudice in his voice stung like a whip. He was so close now she could smell the stench of his breath. A gun waved in front of her field of vision, then a large hand with fat fingers, and for a moment she thought he was going to grab her throat.

She looked up, her eyes scanning his face. Suddenly she was staring through the tinted glasses at the ugly eyes beneath, face-to-face with the man who would stop at nothing to hurt her. The gun tightened in his grasp.

Save me, Lord. I'm about to die.

TEN

"You see this girl, you call me," Doppel-Dex snapped. "Okay? Or I will find you and kill you slowly. I'll kill all of you."

Her breath caught. He didn't recognize her. They were inches away. How was it possible that he didn't recognize her?

Too many people just see a beard or a bonnet, and don't even try to see the person underneath. Jonathan's words floated in the back of her mind.

Her gaze dropped back to the ground. Doppel-Dex swore at them and walked off. *Thank You, Lord!* Suddenly she felt she was able to breathe again.

"Come on," Amos said softly. "Let's go."

Amos offered an arm to steady her and help her up, as Miriam grasped her hand and helped her the rest of the way. Amos climbed up into the buggy and they drove in silence through the small town. He dropped the family off at a small farm on the outskirts of town, where a large, bearded Amish man promised Amos he'd keep Miriam, Rosie and the twins safe until he returned. Celeste hugged each of the women in turn, wondering how she could feel so much care and admiration for people she'd only just met.

"Travel safe," Miriam said, embracing her with the kind of protective hug that she hadn't felt since her mother had died. "May God go with you."

"And with you," Celeste said. She looked from mother to daughter. Words that she didn't know how to say filled her heart. "Thank you!"

She and Amos returned to the buggy and started driving back toward town. As they drew toward the shop, she saw an Amish man, tall with broad shoulders and a straw hat, standing by the road, holding a large picnic basket. Amos slowed to a stop. The man looked up. Dark eyes met hers and she felt something surge in her heart. It was Jonathan, and for the first time the reality of what he'd said hit her for real. This was his past. These people were his family. He climbed into the buggy.

"I called my boss and the police," he said. "They know the criminal who looks like Dexter is here and are converging to find him. Hopefully, he won't slip the net this time." He looked over at his brother. "Thank you for keeping her safe," he said.

Amos simply nodded. He flicked the reins, and the horse started trotting. "There was some trouble, but thanks to *Gott*, we were safe."

"What kind of trouble?" Jonathan's worried eyes searched Celeste's face.

"We saw Doppel-Dex," she said. "He confronted us as we were getting in the buggy."

"I'm so sorry," Jonathan said. His hand took hers and squeezed it. "Are you all right? Is everyone okay?"

Tears swamped her eyes. She'd barely been managing to hold them back, but the concern in his voice and the touch of his hand had somehow let them flow. She nodded. "He said someone had seen me go into the thrift store. He threatened us. But he didn't recognize me! He was right there. In my face, waving a gun at us, and he didn't recognize me. It's like he didn't look close enough. It was like he couldn't see beyond the bonnet."

"Thank You, *Gott*..."

The prayer moved simply and quietly over Jonathan's lips, like hidden water moving beneath the rock. They lapsed into silence as the buggy left town and pulled out onto the high-way. She felt Jonathan beside her on one side and his brother on the other, two such different but similar pillars of strength. She had so many questions. She didn't even know where to start asking any of them; all she could do was pray.

The journey took longer than she'd expected. Despite the fear burrowing inside her and the odd tension between the brothers, after a while she found herself settling into the rhythm of the buggy and the soothing clop of the horse's steps in the snow. It was peaceful in a way she couldn't place, and again she felt the odd longing for a place she'd never known or seen move through her. She found herself very aware of the sound of the horse breathing and the way its flanks rose and fell. Despite everything that had happened, for the first time in as long as she could remember, she felt at peace.

Would there be any of this in the place where Jonathan was taking her? Would there be trees and rolling hills? Or would she be in a square of concrete walls, looking out through her window at more buildings and concrete?

Lord, I know all that matters right now is my safety and I don't even know what I'm asking. Please just reassure me that You still have a plan.

After a while Amos flicked the harness and said something in Pennsylvania Dutch. The buggy turned right and went down a long driveway. A smattering of buildings appeared at the end, what seemed to be a house, a couple of barns and a garage. Then she saw a few vehicles gathered around it.

"Wait here," Jonathan said. "I'll only be a moment."

"Okay." She nodded.

She searched his face, her eyes seeking out his for reassurance. But he didn't meet her gaze. Jonathan and Amos walked side by side to the farmhouse with the gait of two men who were each inside his own world. She was left alone with the horse, standing there quiet and content, as thick flakes of snow swirled down around them. She tucked a warm blanket around the soft fabric of her skirt, finding the clothes much warmer and more comfortable than she'd expected.

I feel so lost and confused right now, Lord. Am I still within Your hand? How is all of this part of Your plan?

After a while, she heard Jonathan and Amos exit the farmhouse, followed by an elderly man clad in a large overcoat and hat.

Jonathan opened the door of a truck and started the engine of a rusty maroon double-cab pickup truck. When it was cleared of snow, Jonathan walked over to the buggy. He reached for her hand and helped her down. She turned to Amos. His shoulders had sagged and there was a sadness about him that made her thankful he'd be back with Miriam and the children soon. She walked over to him and reached for his hand. He smiled and didn't take it, but the kindness in his eyes dispelled every fear she had that she'd committed a social faux pas.

"Please thank Rosie, Mark and Miriam for their kindness," she said. "I cannot thank you all enough for what you have done to help me. I will be praying, every day, that God blesses you and keeps you all safe."

"And we will pray for you," he said. "Travel safely."

She walked to the truck, climbed inside and then sat there with the engine running, watching through the window as the two men paced around each other and shared an awkward goodbye. Jonathan walked back to the truck, and Amos left in the buggy. Jonathan pulled the truck down the driveway. They drove for a while, then stopped at a small gas station and changed back into their everyday clothes. When they got back in the truck, Celeste opened the picnic basket and ate the simple meal of bread, jam, meat and cheese. But when she offered some to Jonathan, he waved her off. His dark brows were knit. The truck shuddered and shook beneath them and for a moment she almost felt the familiar tension headache threatening to creep back.

"It was very kind of the farmer to let us have this truck," she said, grasping for a topic of conversation when she could no longer take the silence.

"He didn't. I bought it," Jonathan said. His voice was clipped. He stared straight through the windshield. His thoughts, his feelings, everything about him seemed locked somewhere far away where she couldn't reach it. "Two thousand cash. More than it's worth but it'll last long enough to get us to the drop-off point."

"Drop-off point? What exactly are we dropping off?"

But if Jonathan heard her question he chose not to answer it. They kept driving. The tension in both her heart and her body grew stronger with each jarring shake and bump. The sun crept down toward the horizon.

"Talk to me, Jonathan, please," she said. He'd done so much for her. He'd saved her life time and again. And what had she done for him? Nothing. There was nothing she could do for him. Even though something about him drew her heart, the same way the breeze rustling in the trees tugged at a deeper longing somewhere inside her.

"Talk to me," she said. "Are you okay? Because you can talk to me, you know. I know we haven't known each other very long, but I'm here and I'm willing to listen."

He hesitated. She waited.

Then he shook his head. "Don't worry, I'm fine."

No, he might want her to think he was fine, but clearly he wasn't.

She took a deep breath.

Lord, I'm really not good at this. I've never been good at small talk or getting people to open up. But I promised You I'd always try to listen to Your prompting even if I didn't understand it.

"What happened between you and Amos?" she asked.

"I left," he said, so quietly she almost didn't hear him. "I was eighteen. We fought. I stubbornly thought I was right and he was wrong. I left and never came back."

Her hand rose to her chest. He'd walked out on his family?

"But Miriam and the children…"

"I never knew they existed until today," he said. "When I chose not to be baptized and to become a cop, I lost everything."

"Is that why you didn't tell me you're Amish?" she asked.

He bristled.

"I'm not Amish," he said. "I was raised Amish but I was never baptized. Being Amish isn't something you're born into. It's something you choose, and not something you choose lightly. It's a commitment between you and God, in relationship with the community. I deeply love and respect the *plain* life. But I've always felt something inside me telling me to work in law enforcement."

She waited, letting the silence—uncomfortable as it was—fill the space between them, with the rattle and shake of the vehicle. She didn't understand how he'd grown up, what he'd gone through or how he could've walked away from his family. She didn't understand what it was about Jonathan that kept pushing her out and pulling her back in again like the beating of a heart or waves gently lapping a shore. But she could listen.

"The story I told you about the day I knew I was meant to be a cop was true," he said. "Every word. I was in Hope's Creek with my mother and my brother when I was about eight and he was seventeen, when some tourists started hassling us because we were Amish. They followed us and threw things at us. They knocked my mother down and gave my brother a bloody lip…"

His voice trailed off. He ran his hand over the back of his neck.

"I was scared," he said. "I was really scared. I was little, and the most important people in my life were being hurt. I balled up my fist and punched back as hard as I could. And they laughed at me and I fell down. Then this car was there, suddenly, beside us with flashing lights and noise. This man and woman stepped out in uniforms with badges and they made the bullies stop." His voice rose. "They protected us. They rescued us. They defended us."

He paused. Silence filled the truck again. The rattle of the ancient vehicle shuddered beneath them.

"That was it," he said. "That was the moment for me. That was when I knew who I was meant to be and what I was meant to do. I was supposed to be there to protect people who couldn't defend themselves. The police had rescued us, and I was going to spend my life doing just that. Rescuing others. But Amos didn't see it that way."

No. From the little she knew of Amos, she imagined he wouldn't.

"How did he see it?" she asked.

"For Amos it was an important lesson that being called to live for God means that sometimes we face persecution," Jonathan said, "and that sometimes walking in God's path for us isn't easy. It was the start of a major fight between us that neither of us could back down from. Maybe we were just too stubborn. Or maybe it mattered so much to each of us that we couldn't see it any other way. But it was a barrier between us that just grew and grew until I didn't know how I'd ever be able to tell him that I felt called to leave. How could I? It was a reminder that we would never see things the same way. See, he didn't blame the bullies for being ignorant or having evil in their hearts. In his mind, they didn't know any better. Still he blamed me for getting angry and losing my temper..." His voice broke. "Or maybe he didn't. But it felt to me like he did. But they were threatening and hurting my mother. What else could I do?"

His voice trailed off again. Suddenly she could see him, in her mind's eye, standing there with his small fists raised. Sudden and unbidden tears filled her eyes.

"I know you don't seem to believe that God calls people to things or that God has His hand on your life," she said. "But I've lost track of the number of times I've seen you call out to God to help us through. I believe, or at least I think, that maybe God was calling you to do exactly what you're doing. Maybe God called you to protect people. Maybe God really did want you to become a US marshal in witness protection. You just tried to go about it in the wrong way."

She didn't know much. She didn't know this man and couldn't begin to pretend she understood his story. But she knew the God he'd read about in the Bible as a child. She knew the God he'd prayed to and called out to. She knew what she believed.

"Do you miss the Amish way of life?" she asked.

He glanced at her sideways. "With almost every beat of my heart. But that doesn't change the fact I know who I am and what I'm meant to be doing."

Okay. Then didn't he hear what he was saying? How couldn't he see what was so clearly in front of him?

"I don't believe God would put a calling

on your heart if it wasn't God's plan for your life," she said.

"I know that's what you believe," he said. "But do you think it was God's plan for your apartment to blow up? Or for you to be on the run from killers? Do you think any of what you're going through is bringing you closer to that house in the country? Because I'm telling you that's not what life in witness protection is like."

Something bristled at the back of her neck.

"Hope doesn't make a person weak, Jonathan. Neither does faith."

"I wasn't meaning to imply it did," he said, then he sighed. "I'm sorry, I'm not good at this. I'm a very private person and I don't like letting people in. So I'd appreciate it if you didn't tell anyone about what happened today. Not about my brother. Not about my past. None of it."

There was something final about the way he said it, like a door had closed somewhere in the air between them.

"Of course not," she said. "I don't know when or how I even would."

"You've been reassigned to US Marshal Stacy Preston," he said without looking her direction. "In a little over an hour we'll reach the drop-off point, meet up with her and go our separate ways."

She sat back on the uncomfortable vinyl seat, sucking in a sudden shallow and painful breath like she'd just had the wind knocked from her.

She was being reassigned to Stacy? Why? How? What did this mean? A dozen questions filled her mind, but only one escaped her lips.

"Will I ever see you again?" she asked.

He shook his head. His shoulders dropped as sudden sadness seemed to sweep over him.

"No," he said. "Probably not."

Oh. She leaned back against the seat, trying to ignore the prickling of tears at the edge of her eyelids and the pain of her breath as it rose and fell in her chest.

God really was closing a door, then. Whatever it was she felt, whatever it was that had nudged her toward Jonathan, God was closing a door, changing her path, and there was nothing she could do about it.

The late-afternoon sun flashed against the windshield, blinding her eyes and pushing the tears closer to falling. She closed her eyes and turned her head away, suddenly feeling too tired to keep them open. She couldn't remember the last time she'd slept, really slept. Jonathan didn't speak. Neither did she. She just sat there with her eyes closed and her head leaning against the vinyl headrest, feeling the uncomfortable springs pressing against her. She wasn't sure how long she drifted in that uncomfortable space between being neither fully awake nor asleep. She felt she'd been fighting sadness, doubt and fear for so very long, and it had finally caught up with her, lapping at her heels, sweeping her over, pulling her down.

Lord, what's going on? Why did You bring this man into my life and why am I feeling drawn to him if he's about to leave?

No, she wouldn't give up hope. She couldn't. Somehow this was all going to work out according to God's plan. Stacy was a wonderful agent and she'd connected really well with her. Stacy would keep her safe. Everything was going to be okay. It had to be.

A car filled her eyes in an instant, small, black and seeming to come from nowhere. Then it hit them with a bang, hard and deafening, seeming to shake the truck and throwing her hard against the passenger door.

"Hang on!" Jonathan shouted. The truck swerved. "Help us, Lord. Save us, *Gott*."

She held on tight as the world shook. They were spinning, flying off the road. Metal screeched. The truck crashed, cutting off Jonathan's prayers in an instant. She looked up.

There was a web of broken glass. Beside her, Jonathan was slumped over the steering wheel. "Jonathan!" Her hand fumbled for the seat belt.

Help us, Lord! Please help us, Lord.

She released the seat belt and turned toward him. The door fell open beside her. Hands rushed in, dragging her backward, clamping a rag over her face and stifling a scream as it tried to escape her lips. Something sickening and sweet filled her senses.

She tumbled backward, feeling herself being yanked roughly from the truck.

Her body hit the ground. Darkness swirled around her, threatening to pull her under.

Jonathan's head ached. Stars filled his eyes and pain pulsed through his body. He slumped forward and the long, loud, wailing sound of a horn filled his ears and echoed through his head. Celeste's muffled scream still hung in the air. They'd been in a car crash, a direct collision with a vehicle that had shot out of a side road, rammed into them and forced them off the road, like someone on a near suicide mission. They'd been thrown into a wild spin as the old truck's brakes had seized. His eyes refused to open. His body refused to move.

Save me, God! I'm helpless! I know I tried to push You away. I know I've stubbornly thought I could live this life on my own. But right now, I can't do this on my own. I need Your help. I need to save Celeste.

Her face filled his barely conscious mind. Those beautiful green eyes huge with curiosity and intellect. The way her hair fell in soft blond waves around her face. The way her fingers felt when they slipped in between his. The way she pushed and challenged him, chipping away at the walls surrounding his heart until he feared they just might swing open. No, he couldn't let the pain win. He had to fight back. He had to push through. He had to save her.

"Help me, God! Help me save Celeste!" His eyes snapped open as the prayer left his lips. He peered through the windshield, watching through the cracks as a young man half carried and half dragged Celeste toward it. He popped the trunk and pulled Celeste toward it.

No! He would not take her.

Jonathan yanked the seat belt away and tumbled from the truck, landing hard on one knee.

"Stop!" Jonathan pulled himself to his feet

and raised his hands with his service weapon clutched steadily in his grasp. "Put her down! Gently! Then get down on the ground! Hands in the air!"

The man froze. He was maybe in his late twenties, with a thin face that had seen more than his fair share of beatings. Jonathan didn't want to shoot him, especially not while he was holding Celeste, but he was prepared to if that was what it took to save her life. Jonathan steadied the gun.

"Don't be a fool," Jonathan said. "You have nowhere to go and I'm not going to let you take her. I really don't want to kill you. Please, don't make me."

Seconds passed. The wind brushed the trees. The setting sun blazed across the horizon. Then the young man crouched slowly and set Celeste on the snowy ground. She groaned softly, stretched and curled up into a ball. *Thank You, God!*

"Hands up!" Jonathan barked. "Step away from her! Now! What did you do to her?"

But as he stepped closer, one whiff of the sweet scene in the air told him even before the criminal did.

"Just chloroform!" The man's hands shot straight above his head. "Small amount! Just so she'd come easy."

"You mean, just so she couldn't fight back!" Jonathan gritted his teeth. Okay, it would take a while to wear off, but she should be okay. The way the man's eyes darted to the skyline and back told him everything he needed to know. "You're a coward. You could've killed all of us, and for what?"

"Look, I don't want any trouble!" The man's voice shook. "I just really, really need the money. And I wasn't going to hurt her. I promise!"

The money. Again, this promise of money had criminals taking foolish risks to hurt her. How could he or Stacy or any US marshal ever hope to protect her from something like this? From desperate people taking foolish risks from every corner to get their hands on her?

"Tell me, how much money is her life worth?"

The man didn't answer.

"Fifty thousand dollars?"

"I wasn't going to hurt her. I promise."

"You drugged and tried to kidnap a woman for fifty thousand dollars!" Jonathan barked.

The man's eyes grew wide. They were glassy and bloodshot. Pity stabbed Jonathan's heart. He was probably an addict. "Yes…sir… I wasn't going to hurt her. I promise! Nothing bad was going to happen to her!"

He wasn't sure who the man needed to convince more, Jonathan or himself. He'd had enough of this. He was going to get his answers right here, right now. "Where were you going to take her? Who were you taking her to?"

"Nobody! I wasn't taking her anywhere!" The man's eyes grew wide. His arms began to bend, but Jonathan's weapon twitched in his hand and the man's arms shot back up again. "I was taking her to a motel room, but not to do anything bad! I promise! All I needed to do was what the website said. I needed to take a video of her, showing I had her, and upload it to Poindexter's website. Then I'd get the money sent to me. Anonymously."

"Then what?"

"Then nothing!" he stammered. "Once the money was in my account, I was going to leave her there, call 9-1-1 and then the police would come get her! Promise!"

No, whoever was behind this would've made him give them his address and wait there until they arrived. Then they'd have killed him. He didn't even want to imagine what they'd have planned for Celeste. He allowed himself one quick glance at her, curled on the ground, sheltered by the warm cloak Rosie had given her.

Hang on, please. Just one moment longer.

His heart ached between the desire to do his job and the need to sweep her up into his arms. Instead, he steeled his resolve. He'd been chasing his tail like a barn cat ever since he'd rescued her from the farmhouse.

"Is it true the same website that has people trying to kidnap her is giving out rewards for taking her picture or posting video of where she is?" Jonathan asked. "And who's behind this? Who's giving the orders?"

The man blinked. "Poindexter!"

"Poindexter is in jail awaiting trial!" Jonathan shouted. "His real name is Dexter Thomes!"

"No, the feds arrested the wrong guy! Celeste was wrong. Dexter Thomes isn't Poindexter. The real Poindexter is out there! He keeps posting updates and instructions!"

That may be what the man believed—Jonathan didn't for an instant. Celeste was convinced that the man she had tracked down, Dexter Thomes, was Poindexter and that was good enough for him.

"Besides!" he added. "Some people online are saying that not only is Dexter Thomes not Poindexter, he isn't even in jail! Police are covering up the fact he escaped! It's all over the dark web!"

How do I protect her from the enemy when the enemy is the internet itself and its ability to exploit people's greed and their willingness to spread lies?

"How did you know where to find us?" Jonathan asked. The man's hand flinched toward his pocket. "Hands up!"

"I was just reaching for my phone!" he said. "I was going to show you! Poindexter's set up a new portal on the dark web for people wanting to win money by helping him find her. Cell phone pictures, video clips, traffic cameras and store security footage. From there it's really easy to triangulate possible locations and hope you get the right one. You know, the typical scavenger hunt stuff!"

How was a US marshal ever able to protect a witness from the entire electronic world?

Jonathan walked forward. "Put your hands on the hood of your car and keep them there. Don't even think about moving."

He advanced slowly, thankful to see the criminal back up as he did so. He waited until he saw him place his hands on the car, then he reached Celeste and crouched on one knee beside her. While he allowed himself only a quick glance at her from his peripheral vision, it was like every synapse in his brain and fiber in his body was keenly focused on her. He brushed his fingers along her face, felt her shudder against his touch and the warmth of her breath. He swept her up into his arms and cradled her there with one hand, while the other kept the gun trained on the criminal.

"Don't worry," he whispered. "I'll get you out of here and somewhere warm soon. I promise."

"Please!" The man shook. "Don't kill me! I just wanted the money."

Him and how many others? And if this man had found them, how soon until the next one did?

"Throw your phone and your driver's license down on the road," Jonathan shouted. He had no choice but to let him go. If he made him walk or handcuffed him in his car, he could freeze to death before anyone found him. And taking him with them where he was going was definitely not an option. Hopefully, he wouldn't make it too far with his car dented and wrecked from the collision. Jonathan had only one priority and she was currently nestled securely in the crook of him arm.

The man peeled out so quickly Jonathan was afraid he was going to spin out again. He fishtailed, righted himself and sped off.

Thank You, Gott.

He holstered his weapon and pulled Celeste deeper into his arms. Her eyes fluttered. Her body was limp in his arms, but her pulse was strong.

"Just give me one moment, and then I'm going to take you to the safest place I know."

He steeled his heart. He was going back to Amish country. He was going to take her home.

ELEVEN

Celeste seemed to be drifting between awake and asleep, from what he could tell. He kept talking to her as he carried her to the car, promising her that when she woke up he'd make sure she was somewhere safe. He laid her carefully in the back seat of the truck long enough to kick the windshield out from the inside. Then he sat beside her in the back seat, cradling her face and neck with one arm while he checked the man's ID.

Steven Penn, aged twenty. What a mundane name and a young age for someone to be in such a bad and desperate place. Poindexter's page was open on Steven's phone, open to a gallery of pictures. He scrolled. There it was, all of it. The location of the farmhouse safe house. Lee's video phone footage of Miller's attempt to kidnap her. Drone photos from the lot where they swapped out the trucks. Cell phone pictures from the diner, which he guessed were taken from the teenager of the electronics-addicted family. Then, finally, the traffic camera where he'd slowed to a stop outside Hope's Creek. No wonder they'd known how to find her. He talked the photos through with Celeste out loud as he looked at them, describing each one in turn. Could she hear him? He hoped so.

"You were right," he said. He stroked her head. Her blond hair tumbled through his fingers. "The diner wasn't as safe as I thought it was, and you were right about the drone. I should've listened to you. I should've told Hunter that you needed to be involved in setting up your own protection plan. We've never faced an enemy like this before. It's not a person—it's a swarm of enemies all connected by one unknown spider manipulating them through the web. I don't know how to fight this. All I can do is run."

He placed a quick call to an encrypted mailbox where he knew he could leave a message for Chief Deputy Hunter undetected. He told her there'd been another attempt on his assignment's life and gave her Steven's full name, social security number, driver's license and license plate. He told her they were going dark, he'd call as soon as he could and he'd keep Celeste safe.

He left her buckled safely in the back seat of the truck, as far away from the missing windshield as possible. He placed the phone under the wheel of the truck and backed over it. Then he turned the truck around and drove back toward Hope's Creek, sticking to back roads and inching along, feeling the cold breeze whipping at him over the dashboard and through the empty hole where the windshield had been.

His eyes cast constant glances in the rearview mirror. He watched as Celeste dozed, lying curled up sweet and peaceful, in the back seat of the truck, her chest rising and falling, and her eyes fluttering, as if she was in a restful sleep just awaiting someone to wake her. He kept talking to her as he drove. Not about anything important. Just stories from childhood, about barn cats and rabbits, and how he'd run down the hill with his brother and twisted his ankle, but stubbornly walked home on it anyway. As sun was setting low beneath the sky, he crested a steep hill and stopped at the top, looking down at the frozen lake that lay below.

"Okay, Celeste, this is where we get out," he said. He put the car in Neutral, pulled the emergency brake and hopped out. Then he opened the back door and pulled Celeste into his arms again. "We need to ditch the vehicle. I suspect Steven is going to get picked up pretty soon and I don't think anybody's going to trace this old truck. But we can't risk it. The last thing we want is someone spotting it on a traffic camera or drone."

"Mmm-hmm," she murmured softly.

She nestled closer to him. The scent of her filled his senses. Protecting her was hardest thing he'd ever had to do in his life, but he wouldn't have traded the assignment for anything in the world. He cradled her to his chest, popped the brake and leaned hard into the truck with one shoulder. The truck rolled slowly down the hill and out onto the ice. The tires skimmed across the surface for one brief moment before crashing through and sinking slowly under the water.

He waited. The wind shook the trees and buffeted his body. He held Celeste tighter.

She whimpered in his arms. "Jonathan? Where are we? What's happening?"

"Shh, it's okay," he whispered. "You're safe. I've got you. We've just got a little bit of a walk ahead of us."

He bent down and pressed his forehead against hers, feeling the softness of her skin and the warmth of her breath. Their lips were so close that all it would've taken was to let himself move just an inch and their mouths would've touched. Instead, he pulled back, feeling something stir inside him, like something long dead coming to life.

Eventually the truck disappeared under the surface. His eyes rose, watching as the setting sun spread long lines of endless pink and gold along the darkening sky.

Help me, Lord, I can't do this without You.

He started walking, trudging across the fields in knee-deep snow, taking one step at a time, with nothing but the bag over his shoulder, the clothes on his back and the woman he was bound to protect held in his arms.

"I'm taking you home, Celeste," he said, not knowing if she could hear him, but that talking to her helped more than she'd ever know. "Back to the house where I grew up. You get to meet my father, Eli, and see the rest of the family again. I'm really very scared about it, honestly. Terrified. See, knowing you've made a mistake is a whole lot different than knowing how to fix it or what to say. I mean, how do you apologize for leaving home for years? What do you say? My father and I have always struggled to communicate. He really likes his silences. And now Mark says his health is failing. My brother put his life and his family's lives on the line to protect us? How could he ever ask them to risk their lives again?"

The sky was an inky wash of dark purple and blue as the farm where he'd grown up in came into view. He'd always heard that things from childhood looked smaller than adults remembered. But somehow it was even bigger—a large farmhouse in the middle with its snow-covered roof and huge white porch, framed by a barn for the horses and another for the buggy and wagon, a hutch for the rabbits and chickens, and fields on the other, ringed by fences and trees. A second, smaller house not much larger than a cabin, had been built beside the main house since he'd left. That would be the *grossdaadi* house where his father lived.

His footsteps slowed as he carried her across the fields, down the long drive and to the front steps.

I'm not even sure how or why I started praying to You again, Gott. *It kind of snuck up on me, but somehow I don't know how to stop. There are so many ways this can go wrong. But Celeste said that if I trusted You that You would guide me. Please help me protect her. I need You now.*

He knocked on the front door. It swung open. There stood a bearded man, with hair white from age and piercing blue eyes. Jonathan felt his head bow.

"Pa, forgive me." He choked on unshed tears he'd never let fall. "I was wrong to leave and I am sure it hurt you to hear I came to town today and did not visit. I don't know the right thing to say to heal what I did. But I'm here for your help. I need sanctuary. I need your help to protect this woman's life."

His father nodded. There was a long pause in which Jonathan could only guess what he was thinking. "*Gott* heals all things in His time." He turned and looked over his shoulder, and it was only then that Jonathan saw Amos, Miriam, Rosie and Mark watching in a silent tableau from the kitchen doorway. "Come quickly. Your brother and this woman need our help."

The smell of something warm and delicious and comforting roused Celeste slowly. She stretched to find she was lying on a bed that was so impossibly soft her body seemed to be sinking into the quilts. She opened her eyes, and it took her a long moment to adjust to the darkness. Then she saw the light of the moon, silver and simple, shining down through a gap in the curtains.

"How are you?" a woman's voice asked.

Then the golden glimmer of lamplight moved through the darkness. She rolled over and saw Miriam sitting on a chair by a low table.

"I'm okay, thank you," Celeste said. She sat up slowly, feeling the grogginess that had kept pulling her under time and again recede to the edges of her mind.

She remembered everything that had happened since the car crash, and yet the memories were fuzzy, like dreams she'd kept drifting in and out of.

The car accident. The abduction attempt. Being chloroformed. The long cold drive before abandoning the truck and continuing on foot. And the stories Jonathan had told her. Dozens of them, it felt like, all about his childhood, his life and his childhood faith, as if the closed book of his life had suddenly opened up and spilled out when she was her weakest and needed something to hold on to in order to keep the fear at bay. Sudden emotion swelled in her chest. He'd been struggling so hard with coming back home, and yet he had, for her, to keep her safe.

Lord, whatever he's doing now, wherever he is and whatever's happening, please guide him and be with him.

"How's Jonathan?" she asked. "Where is he? Is he okay?"

"He's asleep in the chair by the fire," Miriam said. She stood slowly. "He stayed up sitting with Eli, his father, for a long while."

Yes, she vaguely remembered the old man with the white beard and kind eyes who'd greeted them.

"What did they talk about?" Celeste asked.

Miriam smiled softly. "I don't think they talked much at all. Sometimes it is better to sit and be silent with someone when you don't have the right words to say. The Lord moves in silences just as well as He does in words. Now, I brought you some stew, along with some fresh bread, a glass of cold water and another of milk. Jonathan said you would be hungry."

"Yes, I am, thank you." Celeste swung her legs over the side of the bed and was grateful to feel they weren't as wobbly as she'd feared they'd be. "How long have I been here?"

"A couple of hours," Miriam said. "You woke up a bit and I helped you walk upstairs. I made sure you were okay and then told Jonathan to let you sleep."

Miriam set a lamp down. She pulled a small table over beside the bed and placed the tray holding the simple meal on it. As Miriam turned and picked up the light again, the glow cast gentle shadows along her form, highlighting the tight, round curve of her belly, through the thin, soft fabric of her home dress. Miriam followed her gaze, and there was a sweet, almost dreamy quality to her smile. One hand slid protectively over her stomach.

"Yes, Amos and I are having another child this spring," she said. "He always wanted a large family. Rosie and Mark's father died when they were very young, and Amos was so happy to become their *pa*. Then came David and Samuel. Now *Gott* is blessing us with one more."

Celeste swallowed hard. This woman was pregnant, had been threatened by a criminal in front of her children and still had the grace and courage to welcome her into their home. Jonathan had been so right when he'd reminded her not to judge someone by appearances.

"I don't know how to thank you for protecting me," Celeste started. Her head shook. "You don't know me and have no reason to help me. And you've done so much…"

Her voice trailed off.

"Hush now," Miriam said firmly, "and eat, then sleep. We can talk more about your situation in the morning."

Celeste nodded. She started to eat. The

food was warm, hot, soothing and delicious, with tender chunks of beef, along with carrots, potatoes and another root vegetable she couldn't place. There was a quiet to this place and to Miriam that she appreciated. She'd never been good at small talk and always felt socially awkward around strangers. It was nice, somehow, to be able to feel it was okay to just sit there in the peace and not try to find the right words to say.

"This is really good," she said after a long moment. "I've never tasted anything like it."

"It's Amos's favorite," Miriam said. "The baby's, too."

"How did you two meet?" Celeste asked.

"At my shop," she said. "The building belonged to Rosie and Mark's father. His name was Isaac. He said he always felt that God wanted him to use it to help others. He wanted to take things that were unwanted, unused and damaged, repair them, and give them to others who needed them. He wanted to raise money to help people doing God's work overseas. He believed in healing broken things."

Her eyes glanced past Celeste to the window, as if looking at something very far away.

"We moved here as a family, following his dream," she continued. "But he died before the store was open. I was alone with nothing, in a new community and a widow with two small children. Many people were very kind to us. Then I met Amos. He was carrying a lot of hurt and a lot of anger."

"I know Jonathan regrets hurting him very much," Celeste said.

"Three stubborn men living under one roof, all of whom lost the woman who held them together." Miriam shook her head. "Like bulls knocking around hurting themselves and each other. When I met Amos he had such a deep need to love and be loved." Her smile deepened. "We healed each other's hearts. Two months after we met, we were married."

"So quick?" Celeste felt herself gasp and then felt guilty almost immediately. "I'm sorry. I shouldn't judge anybody else's relationship. I've never had what you and Amos have. I wouldn't know what it's like."

A chuckle slipped Miriam's lips, but not an unkind one. It reminded her of the way her mother would laugh under her breath when Celeste complained she would never solve a computer problem just moments before she invariably did.

Instead, all Miriam said was, "Get sleep while you can. I'll make sure Rosie comes in to wake you in the morning and helps you get dressed. In the meantime, there is a night-dress for you at the end of the bed. Sleep well."

"Thank you."

Miriam slipped out of the room, with a rustle of fabric and skirts.

Celeste waited until the door was closed, then set the tray back down on the table and changed into the nightgown. She guessed it was Mark's room she'd been given and wondered where the young man was sleeping. Miriam had taken the lamp with her, but dim moonlight filtered through the window and slowly her eyes adjusted. She crawled under what felt like a mountain of blankets, pulled them up around her chin and curled into a ball. There was something soft and gentle about the darkness and silence that surrounded her.

What time was it? She had no way of knowing. It could be after midnight. It could be as early as nine. Whatever time it was she doubted somehow that she'd have been in bed if she was back home in her old apartment. No, she'd likely be reading a book on her tablet, surfing the internet on her laptop, clicking through social media on her phone or streaming something on her television. Doing anything other than lying still and letting the darkness enfold her. She took a deep breath and let it out slowly, feeling an odd sense of peace spread through her limbs. It was only then she realized with a start that her usual tension headache and the nagging pain she was so used to feeling in her limbs was gone.

Despite the chaos, despite the fear, despite the uncertainly, there was a deeper, more enveloping peace that surpassed her understanding.

Thank You, Lord. I don't know what You're doing. I don't know why I'm here or what happens next. But thank You for bringing me here. Please be with this family and in this home. Help me share this sense of Your love and peace with Jonathan...

She drifted off to sleep with the US marshal's dark eyes filling her mind and his name on her lips.

Celeste was awoken by the morning sun spreading across the floor and onto her face. Then came the sounds of birds chirping, animals baying, the twins running up and down the hall, and dishes clattering from the kitchen below her. She sat up and looked out, feeling her breath catch in her throat at the beauty that spread out beneath her. Prayers of thanksgiving surged through her heart that her mind couldn't even begin to find words for.

A gentle knock brushed the door frame.

"Hello?" It was Rosie.

"Come in." A smile crossed Celeste's lips as the door slid open and the young woman's face filled the doorway, her arms filled with brightly colored fabric. She slipped from between the covers and gave the young woman a hug. "It is so wonderful to see you again."

"You, too." Rosie smiled. "Mamm thought you might like some help getting dressed."

Three dresses hung loose and soft over her one arm, one in peach, one in a bright green and one in the faintest yellow. In the other she held a small white prayer *kapp* and box of pins. She laid the dresses down on the bed. "And our last lesson in how to pin a dress was rather rushed."

Hidden behind a curtain while a criminal came looking for her. Yes, it had been.

She giggled. Celeste laughed.

"Well, I'm very happy we have more time now," Celeste said. Her hands ran over the fabric and let it fall through her fingers. She couldn't believe how good the fabric felt or how lovely and delicate the colors were. She'd always assumed that the fact Amish clothing was plain meant it couldn't also be pretty.

But the simple colors and the way the fabric flowed was more beautiful than anything she was used to.

She chose the green dress, and then paid close attention to every tuck, fold and pleat as Rosie helped her pin it on. After that the younger woman waited while Celeste brushed her hair and curled it into a bun, and then helped her pin her white starched *kapp* in place.

They walked through a hallway and down the stairs to the kitchen. Warmth and clatter rose to greet her, with the smells of sizzling bacon and eggs. They stepped into the kitchen. It was the largest kitchen she'd ever seen, with drip coffee brewing on the wood-burning stove and a long wooden table that she imagined would sit at least fifteen. It was laden with breads, jams, preserves, fruit compote and skillets of eggs and cheese.

Amos, Mark, David and Samuel were so engrossed in their breakfast and happy conversation that they didn't seem to have noticed her. But her eyes were drawn to one man, sitting tall and strong at the side of the table, in a simple white shirt and overalls, his dark hair with a touch of curl bent low over his food. Jonathan turned and looked up at her with a look so simple and honest that it stole her words from her lips.

She then realized the only one missing was his father, Eli.

"*Gude mariye!* Good morning!" Miriam's voice turned her attention to the sideboard, where Miriam stood with a frothy pitcher of milk. "How did you sleep?"

"Very well," Celeste said, her voice sounding more relaxed than she was used to. "I think that was the best night's sleep I've ever had."

All forks dropped and conversation stopped. The men rose, but Jonathan was quickest to his feet.

"Welcome," Amos said. "We apologize for starting to eat without you, but Miriam said we should let you sleep and that you'd probably prefer a more relaxed start your morning."

Celeste felt a smile cross her lips. "Yes, she was right, thank you."

There was a slight pause, then Amos waved his hands and people sat down and went back to eating. All but Jonathan, who stayed standing, his eyes locked on her face with a look so genuine and raw that it was like they were the only two people in the kitchen. Maybe even in the world. He pulled out the chair beside him. She walked over to him. He waited.

"We'll talk later, after breakfast," he said quietly. "How are you?"

His hand brushed her back as he pulled the chair out for her. They sat. She turned to look at him. How was it possible this extraordinary man was just inches away from her, sharing a meal with her in his family home?

"I'm very good," she said. And she was, in a way she didn't know how to explain or put into words. Here in this kitchen, with people she barely knew, she felt at peace in a way she couldn't ever remember feeling before. That longing in her heart had returned, tugging her toward the place where it belonged. Could it be something like this? A large, warm kitchen with a table full of food? A married couple in love with four children and another on the way? A space filled with people who clearly cared about each other and God?

Conversation flowed cheerfully and happily around the table. David told her that he'd found three eggs the day before and wondered how many he'd find today. Samuel wanted to go sledding. Rosie was excited her favorite horse was going to have a foal.

They lingered over the meal, sitting and talking long after the food was done. When the meal was done, Amos rose to help Miriam and Rosie clear the dishes. When Celeste tried to join them, Miriam waved a hand in her direction, with a smile on her face that was inscrutable yet sweet. "Why don't you get Jonathan to show you around the farm?"

"I'll help you!" David shouted, rising to his feet.

Samuel was only a moment away on his heels. "I'm coming, too!"

Celeste glanced at Jonathan. He looked at the boy's eager faces. A smile beamed across his face and set something alight in his eyes, as if he was seeing for the first time something he'd thought he'd lost.

"I'm sure your uncle Jonathan and Celeste would like a quiet walk…" Amos started.

But Jonathan held up a hand. "I'd love for David and Samuel to show us around. If that's all right with Celeste."

"It's very all right," she said.

The boys yelped and ran for the door, only remembering to pause and clear their dishes when their father waved his hand ever so slightly in their direction. The boys wriggled into their boots and put their hats on. When they dashed outside, two farm dogs raced up to greet them.

"There are a couple pairs of boots by the door," Miriam said. "Take whichever pair fits you best, and we'll pick up some that are the right size from the store later today. There are mittens on the bench. The cloak and bonnet closest to the door are for you."

"Thank you," Celeste said, realizing she'd said the words more in the past few hours than she'd said in her life. "How do I say that in Pennsylvania Dutch?"

"Danke." Miriam smiled widely.

Celeste felt her own smile grow in response. *"Danke."*

She slid her feet into a pair of soft brown boots and slipped the cloak around her shoulders. It was warm and comforting. A gentle blast of cold air made her look up. Jonathan was holding the door open. A warm brown jacket sat around his shoulders, and a wide-brimmed hat covered his head. He reached for her arm.

"It's pretty icy," he said. "Let me help you. The paths can be kind of tricky until you get used to them." Her hand slid neatly into the crook of his arm. She followed him outside. The farmhouse door slid closed behind them.

"I want you to wear a cloak and bonnet whenever you're outside," he said. "I don't think we have to worry about aerial drones here. We'd be able to see them a mile away. But I will feel better knowing that you're as unrecognizable as possible."

She nodded. "Agreed."

Her eyes scanned his form. The simple coat highlighted the muscles of his broad shoulders and chest, tapering down to his abs. Then she blinked as something hit her.

"You're not carrying your gun! Where is it?"

"In a locked box in the shed," Jonathan said. A frown creased the lines between his eyes. "It was the condition my *pa* set. We are welcome in his house and he will protect us. But all weapons have to stay outside."

TWELVE

"Come on!" David yelled, scampering ahead toward the barn.

"I'm coming!" Jonathan replied, and tilted his head toward Celeste. "It's still very hard for Amos and Pa to accept that I went into law enforcement. They are very conflicted." He ran his hand over his beard. "As am I."

He guided her up the path, through the snow and toward the barn, holding her as tightly as he dared. The memory of how they'd arrived, cradling her in his arms and to his chest, filled his mind. If he was ever close to her like that again one day, under better circumstances, he might be tempted to ask if he could kiss her smiling mouth. He knew, though, that having any kind of relationship with her was impossible.

"Why wasn't your dad at breakfast this morning?" she asked.

"I saw him early this morning," Jonathan

said. "He said he needed time alone with *Gott* to think and pray. We shared a cup of coffee before he left. We talked a bit last night. Well, less talked than sat beside each other in silence and watched the fire. He is a good and a very Godly man, but has never been one to talk or say those words of reassurance I needed. When I was younger I couldn't handle how quiet he was, how he was drawn into long silences and never answered my questions. How could he work for hours in a field without talking, especially when my mind was full of conflicting thoughts? It wasn't until I'd lived in the *Englisch* world, with its oversharing on social media and its need for instant gratification to every nosy impulse for information, that I began to understand the value of being quiet and keeping some things inside. Now that he is older and his mind is slower, he talks even less. But he has welcomed me home. And I am not about to change the personality of a sixty-five-year-old man. I guess I will get used to sitting in silence and waiting."

"Do you think he's forgiven you?" Celeste asked.

"He forgave me years ago, even as I was storming out the door."

He waited for her to pry, to ask more questions and to dig away at the broken parts of him he wasn't ready to reveal. Instead, she said, "I'm glad it went well. If there's anything more you want to tell me, I'm happy to listen."

Gratitude flooded his heart, followed by a wordless longing to have this woman by his side, protecting her and caring for her.

The boys reached the barn, pushed the door open and tumbled inside, leaving the door open.

"Wait right there!" David called. "We have a surprise!"

"We'll wait!" Jonathan chuckled, then he turned to Celeste. "How much do you remember from the pursuit last night?"

"It's kind of jumbled," she said. "I remember the crash and the man who chloroformed me. I remember you took his phone but let him live."

"I couldn't hold him," Jonathan said, "and wasn't about to let him freeze to death. So I let him go and called Deputy Chief Hunter from his phone. Then I disposed of both the truck and the phone."

"I remember all that, but it's cloudy," she said. "He had pictures of me, right?"

"Someone calling themselves Poindexter has set up a website collecting pictures and videos of you," he sighed, wishing he could spare her this. "He's paying for each tip he gets. He's offering fifty thousand to anyone who kidnaps you. I don't know why."

"I do," Celeste said. "Dexter doesn't know how I found him. He doesn't know how I beat him and how he was hacked. If he kills me and I don't testify at trial, he'll get away with the theft. But he'll always know he lost to me and he'll never know how. If you let me create an encrypted server and go online, I could review the website data and tell you who's running it and who's behind it."

He shook his head, watching the light dim in her eyes as he did so.

"I'm sorry," he said. "I wish I could. I really do. But it's not safe."

Her gaze dropped to the snow beneath their feet. "I wish you believed I could do it."

"Oh, I do believe in you, Celeste." His voice dropped. His hand brushed her chin and tilted it up, until her eyes were looking into his. "I have complete faith in your abilities and I wish I had believed you sooner. I know if anyone can figure out who's running Poindexter's website, why we have Dexter Thomes's doppelgänger running around and where the stolen money is, it's you. But it's not safe. Not with the tools they have at their disposal and the bounty they've put on your head."

Her eyes searched his face. She was just inches away from him. The warmth of her breath tickled his cold skin. He wanted to wrap his arms around her waist and pull her to his chest. He wanted to tell her that she was brilliant and impressive, and he believed in her calling to do what she did with computers just as much, or even more, than he believed in his own to be a US marshal. And more than anything he wanted to admit just how very much he wished he could kiss her.

"Come on!" David called. "We've found the kittens!"

"We're coming!" Jonathan stepped back like a man waking up from a dream. He steeled his resolve. He didn't know how, but he was going to make things right for her. He needed to. "I'm going into town with Amos this afternoon. He says there are some disposable phones that have been donated to the store. I'll use one to check in with Chief Deputy Hunter. And I need you to stay here."

"But it's not safe!" she said. "What if Doppel-Dex is still stalking Hope's Creek? What if he recognizes you?"

He shrugged. "That's risk I need to take.

But I don't think he will. He doesn't seem focused on finding me, just you."

He tried to pull away from her arm, but still she could feel her heels digging into the snow. "Wait! I want to stay with you. I don't want us to split up and either of us go off alone."

"I know," he said. "But I can't be by your side every hour of the day, and you were supposed to be assigned to a new agent soon. Miriam, Mark and Rosie will stay home today. If they see anyone coming, they'll hide you in the cold cellar. Trust me. I won't be gone long, and you will be safer staying here than coming into town."

How could she trust she was safe somewhere without electricity or even a telephone?

Lord, You brought me here. Help me trust in You.

It was hours before Jonathan and Amos left to go into town. She didn't know quite how long or even how to tell time without incessantly glancing at her phone. But it was long enough that she was able to play with the barn kittens, pat the horses and then get a long explanation on how cows and pigs had to be kept at opposite ends of the barn because, as Samuel put it, they "weren't friends." Then it was a trip to the henhouse to meet David's favorite chickens. When she returned to the farmhouse, Miriam taught her how to bake fresh bread for lunch, before taking her on a tour of the pantry and cold cellar to choose pickles and preserves for lunch.

It wasn't until the sun had already crested the sky and started its descent into the afternoon that Jonathan pulled her into his arms, gave her a long hug and the promise he'd be back soon, then climbed into the buggy with Amos and left. Celeste sat on a chair in the living room by the fire and watched the sky long after they'd gone.

For a while Miriam and Rosie sat with her in the living room. Rosie was knitting what seemed to be a long, thick scarf and Miriam was sewing a quilt for the new baby. Celeste sat, listening to the quiet rustle of fabric and clicking of needles as conversation flowed gently between them like a three-part harmony. They spoke about their farm, the foods they'd grown for the winter and their faith.

The two other women excused themselves to go upstairs, but when Celeste got up to follow they waved her down. She wasn't sure if they wanted her to rest or wanted to talk privately without her. Either way, she thanked them and stayed, enjoying the peaceful crackle of the fire, the rustle of the trees outside and the occasional clopping of a buggy going past. After a while a large cat, orange and impossibly soft, appeared at Celeste's feet and, after rubbing around her ankles, leaped up, curled onto her lap and nudged her hand. She ran her fingers through his long fur, feeling the deep rumble of his purr in her fingertips.

The front door creaked. She looked up to see a short man with a wide-brimmed hat and a long white beard stepping over the threshold.

"I'm Eli Mast," he said. He took off his hat. "I'm not sure if you remember, but we met last night?"

"Yes! Hello!" The memory was fuzzy and yet she knew there was something about the old man that both then and now made her feel safe. She'd started to rise when he waved her back down.

"No, sit," he said, "Zeb doesn't like most people and is very particular about who he chooses to sit with. If he's decided to sit on you, he must have decided you're something special."

He hung his hat on a peg by the door and settled into a chair. But it wasn't until his blue eyes, filled with a strength and wisdom that belied his age, fixed on her that she saw the resemblance between father and son. They sat without speaking for a while, watching the flames dance against the wood.

"So, you are the woman who brought my son home to me," he said.

A sudden flush of heat rose to her cheeks and she raised her hands to cover it. No! It wasn't like that at all. Oh, how to explain it?

"I'm a witness in an important court case involving computers," she said slowly. "And your son Jonathan is a US marshal whose job it is to protect me."

"Yes, yes, I know," he said. "You used the internet to solve a bank robbery and now the robber is using the internet to get people to come after you."

She felt her lips part slightly in surprise and closed them quickly before it showed. "That's pretty much it, yes."

"I know the outward circumstances of what brought you here," he said. He ran his hand down his long beard. He spoke quietly, like someone who knew he was nearing the end of his life and was trying to make every word matter. "But the Lord isn't about outward circumstances now, is He?"

She shook her head. "No, I don't believe He is."

"I've been praying for a long time that *Gott*

would return my son to me at the proper time. Now you're here."

Yes, that was what she wanted to believe to. That God had brought her here. That this house, this home and his family were part of God's plan. And that somehow, in some way, God's plan included Jonathan—the handsome, amazing and broken man her heart was being drawn to deeper and deeper the more time they spent together. Did she risk hoping for that? And what if she did give her heart over to hope, and that hope was dashed and her heart was broken?

How would Eli feel when his prodigal son retrieved his gun and left again? How would she feel when she left this place, and went with Stacy to settle into her life in the city and never saw Jonathan again?

"You don't believe God directs our lives?" Eli asked.

Oh, how could he be asking her that at the very moment when she was so close to having everything she'd ever wanted and yet knowing it could never be hers?

"I believe that God has a plan for my life," she said. "I believe God is calling me somewhere. But if it has anything to do with my being here, I don't see how."

The man nodded, and for a long moment he

didn't say anything. Then, when he'd paused so long she thought he'd drifted off or given up the conversation, he said, "My grandsons told me they showed you my garden today."

"They did." It was one of many things they'd pointed out to her while running down the path.

"See any potatoes, did you?" he asked. "Or carrots? How about pumpkins?"

There was a twinkle in his eye that hinted at the younger man he'd once been.

Celeste found herself smiling. "No, all I saw was snow."

"But still you believe there was something planted under the icy ground that would grow there in the spring?"

Her smile grew wider. "Why, yes, I believe I do."

Where was he going with this? Before she could ask, the front door opened. Amos came in, shaking the snow off his boots, then David and Samuel rushed toward him, followed by Miriam just two steps behind them. The boys ran to greet Eli, and she smiled as he turned his smiling eyes toward his two young grandsons. The cat leaped from her lap. She stood up and stretched, excused herself from the happy babble of conversation and walked into the kitchen.

Yes, Lord, I can easily believe that there's a garden underneath that snow. That the trees will bud come springtime and that apples will grow in the fall. That corn, potatoes and wheat are going to burst out of the ground. What do You want me to take from that, Lord?

The kitchen door opened slowly. She spun. It was Jonathan, snow covering his hat and dusting his broad shoulders. There was a cardboard box in his hands, large and damp from the snow. They stood there for a long moment, looking at each other, her lips not even knowing what words to form.

"You're back," she said.

"I am," he said. He knocked the snow from his boots and crossed the kitchen floor. "I brought you something."

He set the box down on the table, then stopped, pulled off his hat and hung it up by the door. She pulled the lid back. It was printer paper from an old-model dot-matrix like she'd had back in early childhood, with little holes down each side of the page from where they'd attached to the printer, and the pages connected at the bottom, end over end in one long, endless stream. She lifted the first page out. Her fingers slid over the tiny letters and numbers, almost unable to believe what she was seeing. "It's Dexter Thomes's code."

"Yup." He pulled off his gloves and set them on the table. He was shifting his weight from one foot to another with the same nervous stance of a boy who'd brought a girl flowers. "Amos had an old printer in the shop that had been donated and was considered too old for anyone to use. The system was so old I didn't even know if it would work. I printed as many pages as I could before we ran out of paper and ink. But it's a start."

"It's amazing, thank you." Her fingers ran down the page, her mind coming alive like a computer booting to life. "I can definitely start on this. And who knows, maybe by the time Dexter Thomes's court date comes…"

"That's the other thing I have to tell you." He crossed the space between them and reached for her hands. She set the paper down and let him take them. They stood there with his hands holding hers for a long moment. She looked down at their linked fingers. There was something so natural and comfortable about it. Was Eli right? Had something been planted? Was this part of God's plan?"

"Dexter's lawyer has launched an appeal based on the fact somebody has Poindexter's website up and running. His lawyers are trying to claim that means you identified the wrong man."

"That's impossible." She shook her head. For a moment, her fingers started to pull away from his.

"I know." He tightened his grip on her hands. "But it means you have to be in court in a little under four weeks to testify against him."

Four weeks? The words hit her like a punch to the gut. But the trial hadn't been scheduled until March.

"There is no way I'll be able to analyze all of Dexter's data that fast. Not without access to the internet. And if I go into the court case blind, without having proved where the money went, there's too big a risk he'll be let go and set free." And something told her that if that happened he'd never stop looking for her and she'd be in hiding forever. "How will I even find time to work on all this data if I'm busy settling into a new life in witness protection? Stacy will barely have time to help me integrate into my new life before I'm yanked back out again to go to court."

Unexpected tears rushed to her eyes as frustration and sadness battled with the sheer exhaustion of the past few days. Would she even have the same cover life before and after the trial? Or would she have four weeks in one strange place before turning around and starting over again somewhere new?

And just how many hours will it be before Stacy arrives and I have to say goodbye to this place and to you forever?

His fingers brushed the tears away, tracing the lines of her face and tilting her head with her tear-filled eyes up to meet his.

"I can't help you with the data," he said, his voice deep with emotion in a way she'd never heard it before. "Hunter will not budge one iota about you going online or having access to electronic devices, even if I'd been open to it, which I'm not. But I do have what I hope is good news. I talked to Hunter, Stacy and Karl, and we've all agreed. The safest place for you is someplace where no electronic device, cell phone or security camera can find you. We're delaying settling you into your new life in Pittsburgh until after the trial. You're going to spend the next four weeks living here, like the Amish, with me and my family. What do you say?"

THIRTEEN

Happiness filled Celeste's heart like a cherry blossom tree bursting into bloom. Suddenly she found herself throwing her arms around Jonathan. She hugged him hard. For a second she felt him resist, like he wasn't sure what to do. Then she felt his arms, strong and warm around her, pulling her close and holding him to her. And for a long moment she just stood there, thankful for his embrace, thankful they weren't about to be separated and thankful for him.

"Sorry, I didn't mean…" she started, not quite able to believe she'd just thrown her arms around him like that, or that he'd responded and hugged her just as tightly. She let her arms fall to her side and stepped back. He loosened his grip on her body, but to her surprise, he didn't let her go completely. Instead, he stood there with his hands resting gently and protectively on her lower hips. "Ever since I found the code that traced back to Dexter Thomes and proved he'd stolen the money, everything in my life has been such chaos. It's like I've been tossed and thrown around in a hurricane never knowing what's going to happen from one second to the next. The idea I could actually spend the next few weeks somewhere peaceful, quiet and safe with people like these..."

And a man like you...

Her voice trailed off. It was the closest thing to joy she'd felt in a long time. Temporary happiness, she reminded herself. Still, she'd enjoy it every moment that God allowed it to her.

"Are you sure it's okay with your family?" she asked.

He nodded. "I asked them first. I will use a series of disposable cell phones to check in with Hunter and Karl. I'll only check and send texts outside the home, and they'll only call in case of an emergency. I'm going to move into the *grossdaadi* house with Pa. You will stay in Mark's room, and he will move in with his brothers. Pa invited him to stay with us, but he's conflicted about that. I understand. He's pretty protective. But between the new baby coming and Pa getting older, Amos and Miriam need a lot of help around the farm. They see us being here, even for a few weeks, as an unlikely answer to prayer."

"So, you know about the baby?" Celeste asked.

"Yup, I was so excited when Amos told me. I love babies."

She smiled. Her hands slipped up and rested on his arms, and they stood there for a long moment, holding each other lightly while the noise and bustle of the busy Amish farmhouse echoed from rooms in every direction. His dark eyes searched her face, and there was a depth to his gaze like a series of books he only just begun to open up to her, but which she'd now have countless long days and nights to read. Then he let go of her and she stepped back. He ran his hand over his jaw.

"Not sure I'm all that thrilled about having to shave, but only married Amish men have beards."

She laughed, happiness bubbling up inside her. *Thank You, God!* She and Jonathan would actually have a few short weeks together before they had to finally say goodbye.

Late-January sunshine streamed through her bedroom window, but the morning chorus of birds had barely begun to reach Celeste's ears when it was overtaken by the sound of a door slamming shut. She sat up. Her heart beat hard in her chest as fear poured like freezing cold water over the gentle warm glow she'd woken up in every morning for the past two weeks.

What's happening, Lord? Have Dexter's minions found us? Do we need to run?

Shoving back the quilt, she pulled herself to her knees and looked out the window, just in time to see Mark stride across the field. She sighed. Knowing him, he'd run out the door in a rush, slammed the door by accident and now felt embarrassed about it. But as she watched him stop by the fence, catch a breath and drop his head as if to pray, there was no mistaking the way his shoulders dropped and how emotion racked his frame.

She dropped back down onto the bed as her pulse raced and her heart ached. Mark seemed to love God and his family in a such a raw, genuine and protective way.

While the rest of the family had embraced their decision to hide her, Mark still wasn't at peace with it. It was like the young man couldn't bring himself to trust Jonathan or to shake the worry that his uncle was going to hurt Amos and Eli again. She couldn't even say he was wrong.

What am I doing here, Lord? I love being here so much and I'm really growing to care for this family. But they've all seen so much pain already and I don't want to ever cause them any more.

The last few days living with Jonathan's family on the farm had been like living inside a greater peace and happiness than she'd ever dreamed of. She'd awoken most mornings to Rosie at her door, asking if she needed help getting dressed. Then there were the daily trips to the barn with David and Samuel to collect eggs, milk the cows and feed the animals, and long multicourse meals with the family. She'd spent hours with Rosie and Miriam learning how to sew, cook and speak some words of Pennsylvania Dutch, while Jonathan was out with Amos and Eli, slowly repairing their relationship while they worked side by side.

At night she'd sit quietly by the fire, going over Dexter's code with a pencil and eraser, looking up to see Jonathan's keen eyes on her face as she slowly found and unraveled the patterns that she saw, in the hopes of finding something before the trial. Day by day, the tension that she'd gotten so used to living with faded from her limbs, along with that nagging headache no pill had been able to rid her of.

Yet, like a small jarring rock in the bottom of her shoe, she'd never been able to shake the knowledge that one day soon she and Jonathan would be leaving.

The knock on her door was lighter and more timid than usual.

"Come in." Celeste swung her legs over the edge of the bed. Rosie's face was pale. "What's wrong?"

"Papa found Mark with a cell phone," Rosie said. "He said he took it from the store because he wanted to find out if Jonathan was telling the truth about you."

Jonathan stood in the kitchen, watching through the window as his nephew disappeared into the fields. The memory of having been the one to explode in anger and take off running in that very direction burned a little too acutely in his memory.

"What did he find?" he asked. Anger burned like hot coals in the pit of his core. He wasn't even sure who or what it was he was upset at. He'd known things might be tense with his family when he'd decided to hide Celeste here. But he'd assumed that they'd protect her and keep her safe. The discovery that Mark had a secret contraband cell phone had shot a worrying hole through that. "Tell me he didn't let anyone know where she was."

"Of course not," Amos said. Jonathan didn't turn, but he could feel his older brother standing behind him. "He says he didn't even turn it on. And I believe him."

But he could have. If Amos hadn't found the phone while the family was getting ready to head out on a day trip to visit friends, who knew what Mark might've seen or done when he'd managed to get somewhere where with Wi-Fi access.

"He is a *gut* young man," Amos added. "He has a good heart. He's just struggling."

Struggling because he can't trust me. And I don't blame him after what I did.

Jonathan ran his hand over his jaw, missing the softness of his beard. Shaving it off every morning was an unexpectedly uncomfortable daily reminder that he'd reached his thirties without a wife or family of his own. And now he was causing unexpected chaos and pain within his brother's.

As if sensing his thoughts, Amos's large hand brushed his shoulder. "This is not your fault, bruder."

"Of course it is." Jonathan turned back. His brother was dressed to go out for the day, with his hat already on his head. Miriam, Eli, David and Samuel were outside with the horses loading the buggy. Forgiveness felt like a choice his brother and father had decided to make, a gift they'd chosen to give him, and each of them in their own way had slowly been figuring out how to rebuild what had been broken. But Jonathan would never forget that he was the one who'd broken it.

Footsteps creaked on the stairs. He looked up, feeling his breath catch in his throat as he met the gaze of the woman standing one step behind Rosie.

"Celeste." He crossed the kitchen instinctively. His hands reached toward her. The morning sun illuminated her features. Did she have any idea how beautiful she was? Or what it did to his heart every time she even just walked into the room? Whatever strange attraction he'd felt that first moment he'd stepped through the smoke back at the safe house to reach for her hand to help her to safety had only grown each moment they spent together. The fact he'd be leaving her life in just two weeks tore at his insides in a way he couldn't begin to understand.

She paused a few steps away from him. Her hand reached for his, and as their fingers brushed it was like, in that moment, everyone else had faded from the room. Her eyes searched his face. "Is everything okay? Mark seemed pretty upset and Rosie said he had a cell phone."

He let his fingertips linger on hers for a moment, just a few hesitant inches away from taking her hand. Then he let go and slid his hand over the back of his neck.

"Everything's fine," he said, willing it so as he spoke the words. "Mark was just worried for his family. He doesn't trust me and probably doesn't know whether to even believe the story we told him about who you are and why you're in witness protection. I don't blame him."

"Do you want us to delay our trip?" His brother's voice jolted Jonathan's attention back to the kitchen.

"No." Jonathan shook his head. Amos and Miriam had postponed this day trip to visit a nearby family twice already. He couldn't keep asking his family to put their entire lives on hold for him. Especially since he'd gotten the impression Miriam's pregnancy was taking a greater toll on her than she'd been letting on. Amos had already confided in him that she'd been on bed rest for the third trimester of her pregnancy with the twins. It was good for them to go and spend time with friends while they could.

Still Amos hesitated and Jonathan could read the thought in his eyes. "If Mark comes back…"

The words trailed off and Jonathan couldn't help wondering how many times he'd left his father and brother with that same worry.

"If Mark comes back before you're home," Jonathan said, "I'll speak to him if he wants to talk and give him space if he doesn't."

Amos nodded. They went outside. Goodbyes were said, hugs were exchanged and Miriam gave Celeste final instructions on setting the fire and heating the stew for dinner. Then Amos, Miriam, Eli, Rosie, David and Samuel loaded into the buggy and left.

Jonathan and Celeste stood on the front porch and waved them off until the family disappeared from sight. He turned and looked at her. Her long blond hair was tied back under a dark bonnet that framed her face perfectly. The beauty of the light of the winter morning was nothing compared to the simple lines of her face.

"I'm worried about Mark," she said.

He nodded. "I am, too, but Amos seemed pretty convinced that he didn't even turn the phone on. We've asked my family to take everything we've told them about you on faith, without any evidence at all. Maybe that was too much for Mark. Maybe he was hoping that if he looked you up online he'd discover that you really are one of the good guys."

"Good gals." Celeste's correction came so quickly he would've laughed if it wasn't for the very real worry in her eyes.

"Still, I don't know what to make of the fact that Mark had a secret cell phone," he admitted.

"Neither do I," Celeste said. "He seems like a such a great young man. He stepped into action to save my life back at the store. I don't even want to think about what would've happened if he, Rosie and your whole family hadn't protected me."

"Then don't. Focus on the fact that Amos has faith in Mark." *And let me worry about whether or not my brother is wrong.* He stretched out his arm. "Let's walk."

"Okay." The flicker of a smile returned to her lips. He felt her fingers on his sleeve as she looped her hand through his arm and wondered if she had any idea of the impact that even the simplest touch had on him. They stepped off the porch and walked out into the wintery morning together.

What was it about this woman that made

his heart race like a teenager's? No one had ever affected him like this before. He'd taken the biggest risk of his life and let her into his estranged family. And she hadn't rejected him or judged him. Instead, it was like she'd stood by him as he'd started sweeping up all the broken pieces of his life and putting them back together. Snow glittered and sparkled as it crunched under their feet. Bright turquoise-blue sky spread above them. The curve of Celeste's arm fit so perfectly into his it was like it was always meant to be there.

He'd never risked opening his heart for anyone before, and here he'd been overwhelmed by a fierce, protective need to care for her that made him feel both stronger and weaker than he'd ever been. All he knew was he was dreading the day he'd have to say his final goodbye. His eyes rose to the sky.

I don't even know what to say, Gott. *It's still so hard getting used to talking to You. Just please, make something good of this mess. Bless my family when it's time to go. Be with Mark and guide his heart. Strengthen me to say goodbye to Celeste. Bring the right man into her life to give her the future I so wish I could...*

He sighed, feeling so much more inside him that he couldn't find the words to say.

"Were you just praying?" Celeste asked after a long moment.

"I was," he said. "I've been praying a lot more recently. It's hard not to here, especially around my father. He seems to pray constantly. He's been reminding me how. I never realized how patient a man my father was, or how what I saw as a refusal to talk to me when I was younger was just him feeling lost in his worries about my mother's declining health and then her death. He says God worked in his heart slowly over time after my mother died and I left, chipping away at his stubbornness and teaching him patience. Part of me thinks he's always been that way, underneath it all. He was always very patient with my mother."

He ran his hand slowly over his jaw.

"You do that a lot," she said. "It's like you're trying to stoke the beard that's no longer there."

He chuckled. "I didn't even realize I was doing it. Yeah, I do miss the beard. But Amish men don't grow beards until they're married."

"You could always grow one and say it was part of your cover. We could say your wife is back on your other farm taking care of your children." There was a lightness in her voice that made him realize she'd meant it as a joke. But he felt himself frown. No, he couldn't. Didn't she see that? He couldn't pretend to be with another woman, even an imaginary one, while he had feelings for her. Celeste laughed. "Too bad you didn't think to create a cover story where we were married. Then you could've grown yours out like your brother and father."

He stopped short, pulled his arm away and turned toward her.

"Don't," he said. "Don't joke about that."

"I'm sorry." The smile dropped from her lips as quickly as it had appeared. "I was just joking. But don't people create cover relationships when they're in WITSEC?"

Yes, they did. But the point was that he wasn't about to pretend for one moment he had a relationship with her. He wouldn't— he couldn't—and he didn't even know how to explain why.

Her hand brushed his arm. Her eyes searched his. "Jonathan? Tell me what's wrong. You look upset. If I've insulted you somehow by implying you'd ever pretend to be in a relationship with me, I'm sorry."

That snapped his eyes back to her face. This again. Celeste's nagging doubts that despite all evidence on the contrary she wasn't worth much and was certainly nothing special.

"You think you insulted me?" he asked. "Are you kidding? Any man would be proud to stand beside you and call you his wife— even if it was just a cover story to fool the criminals on your tail."

He shook his head. How did she not get it? His mind flashed back to the conversation they'd had when they'd pulled up to the diner and he'd realized that she had no idea how truly special she was. And now that he'd had a glimpse of her curious and brilliant mind, and her deeply caring heart, it was impossible to the point of infuriating that she didn't realize that about herself. Well, he might not be able to be the man of her dreams, but at least he could let her know that she was worth so much more than she'd been led to believe by the creeps who had trolled her life.

"Celeste?" He turned and grabbed both of her hands in his. His cell phone buzzed in his pocket alerting him to a text message. No, he could afford one second to ignore it. "You're extraordinary. You hear me? You're a beautiful, brilliant and kindhearted woman who deserves more than a pretend relationship, especially with a man like me."

He watched as her lips parted in surprise,

and he jumped in quickly before her beautiful lips could form words.

"I know this isn't the kind of thing someone in my position should ever say to a witness they're protecting," he said. "Not to mention it might seem doubly ridiculous considering we only met a couple of weeks ago. But I couldn't live with myself if I didn't tell you, just once, that you're amazing, Celeste. You're the most extraordinary person I've ever met, and with every moment I spend with you, I see more clearly that you're beautiful inside and out. And if you weren't in WITSEC and if we didn't both know we only have just two weeks left in each other's lives, then I would tell you that you've already touched my heart and I would very much like the opportunity to get to know you better and see where this could lead. Not that I don't think you deserve someone far better than me."

Celeste's mouth opened wider, but no words came out. Then she bit her lower lip. Everything inside him willed her to say something and break the awkward silence following his admission.

The phone in his pocket buzzed again with another text message. He had to check it.

"Jonathan, I…"

His phone started to ring. He dropped her hands and stepped back. "Hello!"

"Marshal Mast? It's Chief Deputy Hunter." The familiar voice was clear and strong. "I need you to bring Celeste in immediately."

FOURTEEN

Celeste watched Jonathan's face as he listened to whatever his boss was telling him. Her heart was still racing from the words he'd said just moments ago, and now, before she could even begin to wrap her mind around it, there'd been an emergency call.

She pressed her hand against her chest, feeling her heart beat against her palm. Never, in her whole life, had she imagined that a man like Jonathan would ever say those kinds of things about her. Did he have any idea how much she admired and respected him? How very attractive she found him? Or how much it had meant to her that a family as amazing as his had accepted her with open arms?

"Okay. Understood. We'll check in again once we've cleared Hope's Creek." He hung up the phone. Then he looked down at Celeste. "Dexter Thomes's lawyer filed an emergency appeal. Someone leaked that you thought you'd seen him out of jail, and they're trying to use that to say that you might not be a cognitively reliable witness. The judge has agreed they can call you in for questioning."

In other words, Dexter Thomes's lawyers were going to use the fact that a criminal who looked like him had come after her to prove she was nuts and didn't know what she was talking about. A shiver spread through her limbs that had nothing to do with the wintery cold. "When?"

"Tomorrow."

"But I'm not ready!" she said. "I've barely made a dent on the data. I mean, I've isolated some birth dates, but I don't know what to make of them. I was counting on having another two weeks. Plus, I promised Miriam I'd have dinner ready for them when they got home tonight. How soon do we have to leave?"

"Right now," he said. "I mean, we can talk quickly for a few more minutes if it helps get your head around things. Ten tops. Then we have to head back to the house, get changed back into *Englisch* clothes, pack up and go."

"We'll come right back, right?" She tried to convince her lips to smile. There was no way this was as bad as it sounded. There had to be a glimmer of hope, a silver lining, somewhere. "After all, Miriam and I are supposed to be having a quilting lesson tomorrow. And I promised the twins I'd help them name the barn kittens."

Her attempt to lighten the mood fell flat as she saw the sadness move across his face.

"We won't," he said. "I'm sorry, but this is it for this cover story."

He couldn't be saying what she thought he was saying. This was so much more than a cover story. This was a family. This was more happiness than she'd ever known and a glimpse of a life more wonderful than she'd ever dared hope for.

"But what about saying goodbye?"

"There is no time for goodbyes. I'm sorry. We'll leave a note, of course. We have no way of contacting Amos and Miriam, and we can't just hang around at the farmhouse waiting for them. We don't have the time. Karl and Stacy will meet us just outside Philadelphia. The four of us will stay in a hotel under assumed names. Tomorrow you'll testify at the emergency appeal. Then you'll continue on to your new cover life in Pittsburgh."

The fact he'd said "you" not "we" hit her even harder than the knowledge these were her final moments living as the Amish.

"Am I still going to be reassigned to another marshal?"

He shook his head. "I don't know."

"Am I going to be saying goodbye to you tomorrow?" she pressed. "Is this our last day in each other's lives?"

"I don't know." Jonathan's voice cracked, a pain moving through it that seemed to call to the ache inside her own chest. Then she felt the warmth of Jonathan's hands on her shoulders. He pulled her closer. "But here's what I do know. I know that I have faith in you. I know that you're going to be great. I know you're going to get up on that stand tomorrow and convince everyone that Dexter Thomes is Poindexter and you identified the right man. And then you're going to walk out of that courtroom, head held high, knowing you've done everything you could do. I know that, no matter what happens next, you're going to have an amazing life."

She turned her face toward him, feeling dozens of words she'd never say cascade through her mind like text rolling rapidly down her computer screen. What kind of life could she possibly have if it meant never seeing him again? He had no idea what his confidence in her meant to him or just how hard it had hit her heart moments ago, when he said that if circumstances were different he'd have wanted a future with her.

There's nothing my heart wants more than a future with a man like you.

No. Not a man like you. You, Jonathan.

You and only you.

"You're the bravest woman I've ever met," he said. "You're so smart, so strong and capable of so much. You just need to have the courage to see who you really are, step out in faith and be that person you were made to be."

Well, she didn't feel brave, she didn't feel strong and she had no idea who she was meant to be. But she knew that any second now his hands would leave her shoulders, they'd head back to the farmhouse to pack, this moment alone with Jonathan would be over and she might never get another one like it in her life. Her heart quickened, like she was standing on the edge of a diving board waiting to take the plunge, or like it had in the moment she'd decided to put everything on the line to pursue Poindexter online.

She took a deep breath, stood up on her tiptoes and slid her arms around his neck.

"I don't know how to say what I want to tell you right now," she said. "I know we've only got seconds, and I'm more than a little afraid of saying this all wrong. I really like you, Jonathan. I like you so very much. And I really wish this time we've had together here didn't have to end."

His eyes darkened. "Me, too."

She risked taking another step toward him and found herself standing on the tips of his boots. He smiled. Then she felt his hands slide down her back. He pulled her into his chest. She stretched up onto the very tips of her toes. He bent his face down toward her. They kissed. Their lips brushed over each other and settled there as if they were made to be together.

Then she pulled back and laid her head against his chest.

"I really don't want to leave," she said. "I don't want to leave this place. I don't want to leave your family. I don't want to say good-bye to you."

He stroked her head. "Believe me. I want us stay here every bit as much as you do."

She felt tears building at the corners of her eyes. "But you can come back. I can't."

Slowly, gently, he wiped her tears away. "Don't you get it? It will never be the same here without you."

He took one last look around his family kitchen, feeling awkward in his civilian clothes. His gun sat heavy in its holster. He looked at the remnants of the quick meal of bread and cheese that he'd insisted Celeste try to choke down before running upstairs to get changed. He'd debated keeping them in Amish clothes until they'd made it outside Hope's Creek. But he wasn't about to take his family's wagon and horses without knowing how he'd return them, and it would take about an hour to hike to where Mark had parked the truck. It would be much harder for Celeste to hike over hills in her dress, and once they were outside Amish country the clothing might bring unwanted attention. He didn't know how long it would take until they reached somewhere she'd be able to change. If they slipped through the back door and through the forest, no one should spot two *Englischers* leaving an Amish farm. It wasn't the easiest option, but it would have to do.

He'd insisted they leave only the briefest note for his family—*Sorry, we had to go. Will write when we can.*—telling Celeste that his family would understand and that anything more could put all of them in danger if it ever fell into the wrong hands. She'd taken the pen from his hand and added in her own handwriting, *Thank you so much for everything. Ecclesiastes 3:11.*

"It's from a chapter of the Bible that both

your father and I love," Celeste had said. Then she'd turned away and run upstairs, though not before he could see the tears glistening in her eyes.

A large family Bible sat on a table in the living room, its pages supple from the countless times his family's hands had brushed over it. Part of him wanted to flip it open and read what the verse was that she'd referenced. Instead, he sat down at the table and dropped his head into his hands. He never should've told her how much he cared, and he really shouldn't have let himself kiss her.

Celeste believed that *Gott* called people to things. She believed *Gott* put dreams and desires in their hearts. Well, first the desire to go into law enforcement had burned so deeply inside him that he'd lost his family over it. And now the urging in his chest to hold Celeste in his arms again ached more than he could bear.

The door swung open behind him. Jonathan leaped to his feet.

"So you change back into *Englisch* clothes as soon as my family leaves?" It was Mark. The young man shrugged. "And you brought a gun into my family's home."

Jonathan swallowed back his pride and chose to take a leap of faith and trust the young man. "I'm sorry. We're dressed this way because we're leaving. My boss called. Celeste has to be in court in the morning."

Mark's eyes widened. "You're leaving?"

"Yes, and I'm not bringing Celeste back." Jonathan's broke Mark's gaze. He walked over to the sink, grabbed a cloth and wiped down the table. "I will write letters to both Amos and my *pa* as soon as I can."

"I want to believe you, but I can't." Mark's arms crossed. "What is so urgent that you can't wait even a few hours to say goodbye? Tell me you didn't come back only because you needed something and now that you don't need us anymore, you're leaving."

Jonathan opened his mouth, the desire to defend himself threatening to overpower the decision not to. The truth was far more complicated than that. He'd left because he had felt he had to. He'd longed to return for years. And, yes, Celeste had been the reason, but Mark would never know how hard it had been to walk up that front porch and knock on the door.

Before he could speak, footsteps creaked on the stairs, followed almost immediately by Celeste's voice. "Mark!"

Mark's arms unfolded. He nodded to her. "*Gude mariye*, I hear that you're leaving."

"We are." Celeste crossed the floor. She was dressed in her blue jeans and sweatshirt, but her hair was still tied back in a bun as it had been under her *kapp*. "Please tell everyone in your family goodbye from me and how very sorry we are to leave this way. Unfortunately, I have to be in court tomorrow and we couldn't wait."

"I will." The young man nodded slowly as if his brain was processing. He turned to Jonathan. "How are you going to get back to your truck?"

"On foot."

"I will take you in the wagon," Mark said. His chin rose. It wasn't a question. "It will be much faster than walking."

Jonathan rocked back on his heels. On the one hand, the wagon would be much faster. But would it really be safer? Though it was clear his brother believed in Mark and trusted him, Jonathan had never found it easy to take anything on faith. Seemed he and his nephew had that in common.

Mark cut his eyes to Jonathan as if reading the doubt in his gaze. His arms crossed.

"I still don't trust you, and I don't think you trust me," Mark said. "But my faith teaches that I have a responsibility to take care of strangers and those in need, even when it's hard. And I know it would hurt my family if they found out I had an opportunity to help you and turned my back on you. Even if you turned your back on them"

Then Mark turned to Celeste. Something softened in his face, and for a moment the seventeen-year-old somehow looked both very grown-up and very young.

"My friends tell me that you are a very good person. They say you risked your life to help thousands of people who'd been robbed and stopped a very evil man. I was stubborn. I didn't know what to think when I realized you were here with my uncle. I took one of the phones from the store so I could look you up and decide for myself. But, after praying, I decided that I didn't need to go to the internet. I could trust my friends and my family and my faith."

"Thank you," Celeste said, stepping forward before Jonathan could say anything. "I believe you and I'm thankful for your help. I'm sorry for whatever happened this morning, but I'm glad that you stayed home and that God brought you home at the exact right moment to help us."

Jonathan gritted his teeth. It was fine for Celeste to decide she trusted Mark or even to view what had happened that morning as part of God's plan. But what evidence did she have really? What was it based on? The fact he'd helped her back at the store? The fact Mark's family believed in him? The sincerity in Mark's eyes? Despite the fact that Celeste and his father, Eli, were so very different on the surface, they both looked at the world through the same lens of faith. They both had this crystal clear belief that God talked to them and guided them. Well, he didn't have the luxury of believing the same thing.

His cell phone buzzed. He glanced down, and as he read the text from Karl he heard himself groan. He ran his hand over the back of his neck.

"What's wrong?" Celeste asked.

"Whoever's running Poindexter's site has put out a call for people to patrol the roads in certain parts of Pennsylvania, including Hope's Creek," he said. "They're offering double the reward for anyone who manages to spot you and stop you from making it to trial. Also, they've located my truck. We're trapped."

FIFTEEN

Celeste lay flat on her stomach in the back of the wagon, hidden under several layers of blankets, feeling the rock and jostle of the boards beneath her. It had taken only moments for Jonathan to decide that Mark's offer was the best way out of Hope's Creek undetected. He'd fired off a message to Karl and got a pickup location for a new, fresh vehicle, almost an hour out of town, while Mark got the wagon hitched and Celeste had hidden their belongings in the back. The whole thing from Karl's first text to pulling out in the wagon had taken under fifteen minutes.

Since then, though, the minutes had stretched, long and unending, with nothing but the sound of the wind whistling in the trees, the rattle of the wheels and the clop of the horses on the road beneath them, as Mark drove the wagon slowly and steadily out of Hope's Creek. This was probably the slow-

est getaway escape imaginable. The thought
would've made her laugh if it wasn't for the
doubt and fear gnawing in her core, which
seemed to intensify every time the wagon
slowed or she heard someone calling out to
Mark in greeting.

*Lord, I'm so scared. This is all starting to
feel very real. Be with us. Calm my nerves.
Help me to get to court safely. Help me to be
strong on the stand.*

She felt a warm hand brushing hers in the
darkness as Jonathan stretched out for her
from his hiding place on the other side of the
wagon. His fingers wrapped around hers, enveloping them and holding them tightly. She
squeezed him back with all her might. Then
she let herself relax. For some time they just
lay there, side by side, their hands linked in
the darkness.

Finally, she felt the horses slow.

"Okay, I think this is the place," Mark said.
"But it's just an abandoned junkyard."

Jonathan's hand pulled away from hers.
She felt him shift his position in the back
of the wagon beside her. A glimmer of sunlight slipped in through the blankets as Jonathan peered out. She moved onto her side and
glanced through the gap, but saw nothing except the pale blue of sky ahead.

"Do you see anyone?" Jonathan asked.

"No one." Mark's voice filtered through the blankets from the front of the wagon. "This place is empty."

She heard Jonathan breathe what sounded like a prayer of relief under his breath.

"There should be a red pickup by the back fence, with California plates and a rack on the back," Jonathan said. "Pull up beside it."

"Got it," Mark said.

For a moment there was only the sound of the horse-drawn wagon moving over the snow. She reached out for Jonathan's hand again but couldn't find him. The wagon stopped. She felt the blankets move back and saw the mixture of lights and shadows shift as Jonathan crouched up. "Looks good."

She scooted onto her knees so she could see, then felt his firm hand on her shoulder gently pushing her back down.

"Stay down," he said. "Wait here. I need to check out the truck and the surroundings."

"Okay, be careful," she said, but wasn't sure he'd even heard her before he'd hopped over the side of the wagon. She lay back on the cold floor, closed her eyes and prayed. Something about Jonathan's warm and tender touch had filled her with so much hope. Feeling him pull away made her feel like part of her was missing. She needed to get a hold of her heart. Jonathan was not a permanent fixture in her life or someone who'd always be there to help her weather the storms. No, he was leaving her life, and soon. The quicker she stood on her own two feet the better.

"Okay, Celeste, you can come out now," Jonathan called.

He pulled the blankets back and grabbed their bags. She looked around. The carcasses of old and broken cars, half buried under the snow, spread out to her right. Tall fencing surrounded them on every side. She pushed the blankets off entirely and stood. Jonathan was carrying bags to the truck.

Mark stood beside the wagon and offered her a hand down. Standing in the snow, she paused, wanting to hug him but also knowing he'd probably feel more comfortable if she didn't.

"I wish I could find better words to say than thank you. *Danke.* Thank you for everything you and your family have done for me."

A slightly sad but entirely genuine smile crossed his face. "You're welcome. Safe travels."

"You, too," she said. "I hope God blesses you all so much for everything you've done for me."

She felt movement behind her and turned to see Jonathan at her shoulder. He nodded to Mark and they exchanged a quick and awkward goodbye. She followed Jonathan to the truck. He unlocked the doors and they got inside. He started the engine, but she remained still, her hand on the seat belt, watching through the windshield as Mark turned the horse and wagon around, and started toward the entrance.

"Everything okay?" Jonathan asked.

"No…" Celeste's voice trailed off.

Something was wrong. Something was gnawing at the pit of her stomach hurting her with each breath, but she wasn't sure what.

The screech of tires filled her ears. A car, brown and streamlined, flew into the parking lot, swerving to a stop in front of Mark. The horses reared. Mark's body jerked as he tried to steady them.

"Get down!" Jonathan slid a protective arm around her shoulder.

A large figure holding a gun jumped from the car and charged toward Mark. Even at a distance she couldn't mistake his form. It was Doppel-Dex. The imposter yanked Mark down from the wagon with one hand. With the other he pressed the gun into the side of Mark's head.

SIXTEEN

"You can drive this truck, right?" Jonathan grabbed her by the shoulder with one hand and turned her to face where Mark now knelt, shaking, on the ground. With the other he pressed a cell phone into her hand. "Celeste! Tell me you're able to drive this truck and get out of here."

Through a junkyard, in the snow, with someone she cared about down on his knees with a criminal's gun to his head?

"Absolutely." She gritted her teeth.

"Great." Jonathan reached for the door. "If anything happens to me, as soon as the entrance is clear, I expect you to gun it. Okay? Don't look back. Just get as far away from here as you can and call Stacy or Karl. They'll send someone to get you."

She felt the quickest brush of Jonathan's lips over hers. Then he jumped from the truck, slammed the door and started toward where Mark now knelt. Her limbs shook as she slid her body into the driver's seat, and she watched through the windshield, silent prayers forming on her lips, as Jonathan strode toward the gunman.

Doppel-Dex shouted, and while she couldn't make out the words at a distance, there was no mistaking the ugly menace of his tone. He cuffed Mark so hard across the face he nearly fell forward. The teenager's shoulders shook. Jonathan stopped walking. His hand twitched toward his gun. Her heart stopped. Jonathan was going to shoot a man in front of his Amish nephew. It was the only way to save his life.

But then the US marshal raised his hands high above his head. A gasp crossed her lips as she watched him toss the service weapon he'd only recently been reunited with into the snow. Could he be surrendering to the one man who'd been chasing her since the farmhouse? Was he offering up his own life to save his brother's son? Jonathan knelt and placed his hands on his head. There was a pause, then Doppel-Dex dropped his grip on Mark's shoulders and turned his gun on Jonathan.

"Where. Is. She?"

She heard that all right. Even at a distance,

those three words snapped in the air like a bullet's crack.

But whatever Jonathan said in response was so quiet she wasn't able to catch the sound of his voice. Mark turned and pelted toward the wagon. Doppel-Dex spun back toward him. Jonathan launched himself at him like a linebacker. The criminal's gunfire echoed in the air above them. The horses whinnied as Mark grabbed the reins and spurred them on. The wagon clattered through the junkyard. Jonathan and Doppel-Dex wrestled for the gun. The wagon cleared the gate and disappeared down the road.

Thank You, Gott. Celeste buckled her seat belt and gunned the engine. The truck flew forward, toward the two men and the open gate beyond. Doppel-Dex tossed Jonathan to the ground. Jonathan reared up, blocking the larger man's blows. She breathed a prayer and yanked the steering wheel to the left, denting the corner of a wrecked hatchback as she forced the vehicle to a stop. She leaned over and shoved the door open. "Jonathan! Get in!"

He jabbed a quick blow to Doppel-Dex's face, knocking him back. Jonathan ran for the truck, scooping up something off the ground as he ran. It was his service weapon. She threw the vehicle into Drive the moment his body landed in the seat, even as he was still closing the door behind him. She aimed for the junkyard exit. Jonathan buckled his seat belt, then rolled down the window, released his weapon's safety but didn't let off a shot. Jonathan growled. "I don't have a clean shot."

She looked up. Doppel-Dex had dived behind a pile of debris. "You want me to stop?"

"Absolutely not," he said. "Keep driving. I'm not going to stick around and play cat and mouse for a criminal in a junkyard. How's Mark? Did he get away okay? I couldn't really see where he went."

"He's okay," Celeste said. "He got away."

"Thank *Gott*."

Funny, the Amish word for God had been the one that had slipped from her lips, too. She reached the gate and took another glimpse at the rearview mirror. Doppel-Dex was scrambling to his car. She hit the road and turned in the opposite direction of the way she'd seen Mark go.

"I told you to gun it and get out of here," Jonathan said.

"I wasn't leaving without you!" she said. The sound of an engine gunning roared behind then. She urged the truck faster. In the rearview mirror, Doppel-Dex swerved through the gates and started after them. She fixed her eyes on the road ahead. Behind her she could hear Doppel-Dex firing. Jonathan shouted for her to stay low. The back window exploded into shards of glass. *Help us, Lord!* She heard the sound of Jonathan returning fire. Then, as she watched in the rearview mirror, the pursuing vehicle suddenly jolted and swerved off the road and into a ditch.

"What just happened?" she asked.

"I shot out his tires," Jonathan said. He reached for his phone and it was only then she realized she still had it, wedged between her palm and the steering wheel, in a white-knuckle grip. She relaxed her fingers. He slid it from her hand. "I'll call it in, and I'll take over the driving as soon as I know we're clear and safe. That was a minor crash. He should be okay."

She focused on driving and waited while he called both Karl and Chief Deputy Hunter. He ended the call and sat back on the seat. He frowned and his brow knit.

"They'll send law enforcement to look for him," he said. "I don't know how big the operation will be."

Holding the steering wheel with one hand, she reached over with the other and brushed the back of his hand, but he didn't take her fingers. "I'm sorry he got away."

"It was the right move," Jonathan said without really looking at her. "I was not about to risk your life by trying to apprehend him when I'm with you. Catching him was not worth losing you. Nothing is more important to me that making sure you're safe and alive. You matter to me. You have no idea how much." His fingers parted, making space for hers. His thumb ran slowly over her hand. She glanced his way, and as their eyes met, something moved through them, so deeply in their core that it was like he was seeing her and she was seeing him for the first time. She shivered. "Celeste? There's something I need to tell you. Something important that I need to let you know. I..."

He choked on the words before he could say them.

She squeezed his fingers. "Jonathan? Is everything okay? Whatever it is, you can tell me anything."

She waited as silence filled the truck and the man beside her struggled to find the words to say. His eyes closed. She watched as he swallowed hard.

Then he pulled his hand away and crossed his arms.

"Never mind," he said. "Karl and Stacy are en route to meet us. They'll escort us to a hotel on the outskirts of Philadelphia where we'll check in under assumed names. Tomorrow, all four of us will escort you to the courthouse. If Doppel-Dex is not apprehended, there's a possibility he'll strike there." His mouth spread into a tight smile. It was an impersonal and professional grin, missing all the warmth and tenderness she'd gotten used to seeing on his face.

He lapsed into silence again. It was uncomfortable, like a walled fortress encasing him that she wasn't welcome to enter, and it made her stomach ache.

She kept waiting, minute after minute and hour after hour for the wall to fall, for them to go back to that natural, easy, comfortable way they usually were together. But even after they stopped to switch drivers, stopped yet again for food, and then finally met up with Karl and Stacy just as that sun was beginning to set, Jonathan's professionalism and silence remained, and that incredible mind and heart she'd begun to care so deeply about stayed out of her reach.

Artificial yellow light filtered through the curtains of Jonathan's rectangular hotel room, clashing with the shining red block numbers of the alarm clock on the other side of his bed. It was quarter to six in the morning. An hour before his alarm was set to go off and two before it was time to escort Celeste to Dexter's trial. Doppel-Dex had still not been apprehended, and law enforcement would be on alert for some kind of attempt on Celeste's life at the trial. Karl lay fast asleep and snoring lightly on the other hotel bed. If Jonathan had managed to get any sleep, his aching body wasn't aware of it.

Instead, his mind had returned, again and again, to that moment in the truck right after he'd made the call to let Doppel-Dex go in order to ensure Celeste's safety.

He'd just been about to foolishly blurt out to Celeste the words he'd never imagined saying to anyone, let alone a witness he was protecting.

I think I love you.

But how could he ever say those words to Celeste? Knowing what a short time they'd known each other? Knowing that it was highly unprofessional and that as a marshal and witness they could never be together? Knowing that she deserved so much better than a man like him? He rolled over onto his side, balled his pillow and tried to punch it into a shape that would fit comfortably under his head.

His family had forgiven him for leaving them the way he had. He knew Celeste would accept him despite it, too, and that she'd tell him God had forgiven him.

Jonathan wasn't even sure if what he wanted was forgiveness. What he felt more than anything was anger. Not freshly angry over something new that had happened. No, this was like a deep-seated anger that had burrowed in him years ago and had never gone away. He'd been angry when bullies had attacked them. He'd been angry when Amos had told him he couldn't be a cop, when his mother had died and when he and his father couldn't communicate with each other. He'd been angry when he'd left home without looking back.

He'd been angry long before Celeste had come into his life. She'd gotten him praying again. She'd gotten him hoping again. She'd been the missing piece that had brought him back to his family and the life he'd left behind. And as much as he longed for a future with her, he knew there was no way it could happen.

I'm tired of pretending I'm not angry at You, Lord! Why did You take my mother from me? Why did You place a calling on my heart when the only way I knew how to pursue it

*was to rip me away from my family? Why did
You let me meet Celeste, and start falling for
her if You were going to take her away again?*

Enough. He couldn't sleep, he couldn't
pray, he couldn't think and he didn't much
like what he was feeling. He opened the
nightstand drawer and found a hotel Bible.
He dropped to the floor on the other side of
the bed, sat with his back to where Karl lay
sleeping and looked out at the Philadelphia
skyline outside. What was that Bible verse
that Celeste had written on the note for his
father? Ecclesiastes 3 something?

He found Ecclesiastes in the middle of the
Bible and started skimming. It wasn't until he
hit the point about there being a time to plant
and a time to harvest that he really started
reading. He'd found it. The section both his
father, the farmer, and Celeste, the computer
programmer, loved so much, about how there
was a time for everything.

And then he read, "He hath made every
thing beautiful in his time: also he hath set
the world in their heart, so that no man can
find out the word that God maketh from the
beginning to the end." And then a couple
more lines down, "I know that whatsoever
God doeth, it shall be for ever: nothing can
be put to it, nor any thing taken from it."

He set the book down and laid his head in his hands and prayed.

Gott, *I don't get what You're doing in my life or what You're making out of me. I know I want the peace that my pa has. I want the joy that Amos has found. I want the hope that Celeste has in You. So, I'm giving up trying to figure it out. Just show me what You want me to do.*

He wasn't sure how long he sat with his palms pressed up against his eyes, or when exactly he'd fallen asleep. All he knew was that when he woke up, the light of the real living sun was streaming down onto his face and Karl was standing over him with a cell phone in his hand.

"That was Stacy," he said. There was a flicker of something in his eye when he said her name that Jonathan couldn't quite read. "She and Celeste will meet us in thirty in the lobby. We have to go. The hearing was pushed up by two hours because of the chaos at the courthouse."

He was on his feet within a heartbeat. "What kind of chaos?"

"When news leaked online that she was going to testify today, people showed up in droves. The courtroom is crowded. There are people gathered outside with signs."

Jonathan stopped short. "What?" People were coming crossing the country to see Celeste? "What people?"

"People who were robbed by Dexter Thomes," Karl said. "People she was trying to help. She may not have found the money they lost, but she stepped up and caught the man who robbed them. Your girl is a hero."

"She's not a girl—she's a woman," Jonathan said quickly. Maybe if Karl learned to be smarter with his mouth, Stacy might one day look at him the way he sometimes looked at her. And Celeste definitely wasn't *his*.

Their phones both beeped. Karl reached his first.

"It's Hunter," Karl said. "Poindexter has posted online that if Celeste shows up to testify, she won't leave the courtroom alive."

SEVENTEEN

"Everything okay?" Celeste leaned toward Jonathan and whispered as they sat side by side in the back of Karl's vehicle as his colleague eased them through traffic and up to the courthouse.

It was a question Jonathan had felt her asking in a dozen different ways—words, looks and gestures—ever since he'd walked into the hotel lobby and his eyes had brushed over her form. It was a question he still didn't have an answer to. She'd looked exquisite, he thought, in a long blue *Englisch* dress with a high collar and a pale blue scarf, the color of the morning sky. Her blond hair was tied back in a loose bun at the nape of her neck.

"Of course," Jonathan replied, knowing that he wasn't really answering the question she was asking. "Everything is fine. Dexter Thomes will be under armed guard, you've been well prepared for your testimony and I'll be keeping you safe every step of the way."

But is everything okay between us? He could read her green eyes asking the question. He tightened his smile and broke their gaze.

No, it wasn't. Because there could never be an *us.*

Guide me, Gott. *I'm trying to trust You have a plan.*

He glanced through the window at the crowded courthouse steps. A sight filled his eyes that was both one of the most incredibly incongruous and yet surprisingly joyful things he'd ever seen—his *pa* and Mark stood on the sidewalk outside the courthouse.

"What are they doing here?" Laughter spilled from Celeste's lips as she squeezed his hand and he let himself feel her there for one long moment before pulling away.

"I honestly have no idea!" He waited for Karl to safely park the vehicle. Then he got out, keeping Celeste close to his side. Stacy and Karl took up protective positions on either side of him and Celeste.

"Pa! Mark!" Jonathan called. The older man and the young man made their way through the crowd, oblivious to the curious looks of some of the *Englisch* as they passed. "How are you even in the city?"

"Mark's friends from the *Englisch* church heard that Celeste was testifying today," Eli said. "When we got back to the farm, he told us what had happened and said he needed to come see you."

"You drove?" Jonathan blinked. While the Amish didn't drive or own cars, many weren't opposed to getting a ride in somebody else's car when the situation required it. Not that he could remember his own father taking a ride anywhere except to the hospital with his mother.

"The *Englisch* pastor drove us in his church van," Eli said. "He is a good man. We talked on the journey. He said he wants to send some of his young people to help volunteer in the shop, and has offered to give Mark a mentorship at the church, helping with the youth program while he decides whether he wants to be baptized. I like this idea very much, and I think Miriam and Amos will, too. It will keep him close to God and home, while he figures out what God wants him to do."

The glow in Mark's smile said that he did, too. Not only did the young man seem no worse for wear after being threatened by Doppel-Dex, there was something in his stance that would've made Jonathan think he'd grown a whole year or two in maturity overnight.

"I'm very proud of you," he said. He suspected that Mark would one day choose to be baptized in the Amish faith. "I am glad to see that you're not repeating the mistakes I made. I wish I had been as wise and faithful when I was your age, and not as stubborn and angry."

"You saved my life." Mark said the words slowly, like he was reading off a thoughtfully written list. "You risked your life for me. You sought peace with the enemy before resorting to violence and weapons. I'm sorry that I doubted you."

"I'm not," Jonathan said. "I'm glad you were looking out for your family, and in a way, you giving me a hard time helped me get my mind and heart straight."

"All that matters is that you're open to God's calling now." Eli clasped him on the shoulder.

"We'll meet you here after the trial," Mark added. "We'll talk more then, Onkel."

Uncle. The word swelled something unexpected inside Jonathan's heart.

They said quick goodbyes, then Jonathan walked up to the courtroom steps with Celeste by his side. It was one thing for his father to tell him to listen to God's calling. But what was God saying? They entered the building, went through security and down a hallway, where they were greeted by lawyers. Then it was time for him to escort her into the courtroom and into the witness-box. They stepped into the courtroom, and for the first time since the ordeal had begun he laid eyes on Dexter Thomes. The hacker sat tall and arrogant in the dock, seeming to somehow project a swagger that implied he'd be sauntering out a free man. His signature tinted glasses were gone, his beard was trimmed and his shaggy hair was pulled back in a ponytail. His eyes tracked Celeste's every motion like a hawk. Doppel-Dex was nowhere to be seen.

"I'm nervous." Celeste's voice was so low Jonathan barely caught it as they approached the witness stand.

"If you get scared look at me," he said quietly. "I have your back."

The trial resumed, and then all he could do was sit there and watch as the prosecutor walked Celeste slowly but thoroughly through every detail of how she'd tracked Dexter Thomes online and why she was convinced he was Poindexter.

A man slipped into the back of the courtroom and took a seat, and Jonathan found his well-tuned senses turning toward him. The man was tall, bald and clean shaven, with a face so hollow it bordered on skeletal. He was fiddling with his phone and something about him sent a shiver of warning down Jonathan's spine.

He nodded to Karl and glanced the man's way. Karl nodded back.

"It's like seeds planted underneath the soil..." Celeste's voice dragged his attention back to the witness-box. "There are always patterns in the data, even when they're hidden so deeply you can't see them."

She sat up straight, her head held high and her eyes focused as Dexter's defense attorney took over the questioning. Despite every assault the defense attorney could launch on her integrity, intellect and judgment, she remained utterly unshaken in her resolve that, yes, Dexter had stolen the money.

"But you told officials that you thought you saw Dexter Thomes in some rural town in Pennsylvania." The defense lawyer smirked. Jonathan bristled. He wasn't even trying to prove that Dexter Thomes was innocent, just discredit Celeste.

"I saw a man who looked like him," she said. "I did not see him."

"Like you saw a pattern in code that nobody else could see," the lawyer said. "And we're supposed to take this on faith?"

He said the word *faith* as if it was a dirty

word. Jonathan winced. Was that how he'd sounded when she'd explained it? For a moment Celeste didn't answer. Instead, she looked at Jonathan. Their eyes met and a soft light dawned in her eyes. A smile crossed her lips and it lifted something in his own heart.

"I believe in the sun even when it's hidden behind a cloud," she said, her eyes on Jonathan's face. "That's not blind faith. That's knowing that something is real even when I can't see it."

Her eyes then turned to the judge.

"Before I went off-line, I downloaded a copy of Dexter Thomes's background data on his site. Over the past two weeks, I've been working on it the old-fashioned way, with a pencil and paper, line by line, trying to find the pattern. Now I know I've finally found one. And if you gave me a laptop right now and access to the internet, I would be able to tell you exactly where the money has gone."

Jonathan blinked. How was that possible? Confidence seemed to radiate through her, taking his breath away. It took everything in his power, all his strength and resolve not to tell the judge to listen. But there was nothing he could do other than listen as she argued her case, as she proved her mettle and her worth, as she shone like a light and explained, in words that were above his head, what she was able to see in the data and why she thought she could continue to follow it to the end. Finally, after a sidebar between the judge and lawyers, somebody brought Celeste a laptop. The courtroom fell silent as everyone held their collective breath and watched her fingers fly over the keyboard, typing, exploring, scrolling and dissecting. Then she gasped.

"And I've done it!" She spun the laptop around toward the judge. "I've found it. Well, I've found him. I've known for a while that Dexter was searching birth dates and social security numbers, but I didn't know why. He was looking for his half brother, a petty car thief called Casper Harrison."

Instantly the smirk fell from Dexter's face as cell phones began to ping around the courtroom. People rustled in their chairs. Something was happening. And by the smile on Celeste's face, he was certain she knew what it was.

Jonathan glanced back to the bald man in the back of the courtroom. He was gone.

"Casper and Dexter look different enough," she went on, "but apparently enough alike to be able to fool people. Dexter stole the money. He sent the money to Casper, who's been using it to pay people off for tracking me, or at least he has been." The chorus of phone chirps grew louder. Even those who'd apparently had the good sense to turn their phones to silent were checking them. "Because I just found the money and sent it back—a simple reverse payment algorithm. I'm guessing the sounds you're hearing are people getting notified by their banks that the money is back in their accounts."

Gasp and murmurs spread across the courtroom, which turned into babbles of conversation, laughter and even applause. Dexter's head had fallen into his hands.

Celeste's gaze met Jonathan's again and held it.

"I also deleted Poindexter's database on me," she said. "Every trace of the pictures and videos that he was using to track me is now gone. More importantly, now everyone in the world will know that he's lost his money and has no way to pay the bounty. So, there's no reason for anyone to come after me or the people I care about. And the money trail I uncovered will give investigators everything they need to keep Dexter in jail for a long time."

A high-pitched siren filled the air as a voice in the back of the room shouted, "Fire! The building's on fire!"

Instantly the voice was joined by a chorus of shouts and screams as people ran for the exits. Jonathan was on his feet and running for Celeste, his single-minded focus latched on her face even as he could hear pandemonium and chaos erupting around them. For one agonizing second he thought she was going to freeze again. Instead, he watched a silent prayer cross her lips. Then she leaped from the box and ran for him. In an instant, he caught her around the waist. His hand slid around her as he steered her toward the closest exit. Smoke poured down the hallway to their left.

"Come on," he said. "They're evacuating the building. We've got to go."

"Wait." She grabbed his arm, and her heels dug into the floor. "What if it's another smoke bomb like back at the safe house? What if it's not a real fire? What if Doppel-Dex is trying to create a diversion?"

He glanced at the docket. Dexter was being ushered out by bailiffs. His head was bowed.

"I don't know." Jonathan steered her into the crowd of people and toward an exit. "But we're not going to hang around here and find out."

A split second that felt like a decade passed.

"Okay," Celeste said. "I trust you."

Thank You, Gott. They joined the crowd and hurried for the exit. Within a heartbeat, Stacy and Karl had joined them, flanking them on either side. They jogged down the hallway, through the doors and out onto the court steps. Sunlight filled his gaze. He gasped a breath and glanced around, then realized who was behind them. Dexter Thomes had been evacuated through the same door they had. He guessed the usual exit they'd have taken him through been blocked somehow due to smoke.

Were Celeste's suspicions right? Was this nothing but a diversion?

"Karl, Stacy." He spun to his colleagues. "I think there's something wrong—"

Before he could finish the thought, something banged and flashed, filling his eyes with blinding light. Voices screamed. People shouted. Thick green smoke swamped the courthouse steps. His eyes flooded. Painful smoke seared his lungs. Someone had set off a smoke bomb. He felt something hit him hard and he pitched forward, almost falling down the steps as the sound of Celeste screaming filled his ears.

EIGHTEEN

"Celeste!" Desperately his eyes scanned through the smoke. Amid the chaos of people and panic, he could hear Celeste's desperate cries still hanging in the air.

Help me, God. I'm blind! Guide me! Show me where to go!

"Jonathan, Karl, I've got eyes on the suspect!" Stacy shouted. "He took Celeste around the left side. This way!"

Jonathan turned and ran toward her, Karl one step ahead of him, as they pushed through the crowd and the chaos. His eyes locked on one form. Dexter Thomes was wrestling with a guard, fighting for his gun. The hacker yanked the officer's weapon from his holster.

"Dexter Thomes has got a gun!" Jonathan yelled.

Help me, Gott. I can't save Celeste and stop Dexter.

"We've got him!" Stacy yelled. "You go

get Celeste." She stopped on a dime and spun toward the criminal. "Drop your weapon!"

Jonathan ran in the direction Stacy pointed. The scene played before him in an instant. Dexter fired. Stacy cried out in pain as her leg crumpled beneath her. She dropped to the courtroom steps, but her weapon was held sure in her hands. She rolled onto her back and fired, Karl's steady and sure bullets joining hers as he ran toward her. Dexter fell, but not before another burst of gunfire escaped his weapon. Karl threw himself between Stacy and the bullets. He wrapped his body around his partner, and they tumbled down the steps together.

Gott, protect them!

He couldn't let himself stop. He ran through the smoke and he saw them, Celeste's blond hair tossed loose from her neat bun and her limbs thrashing as she fought for life against the grip of the hulking, bald man he'd seen in the courtroom.

He was already on his way. He burst through the door and found a long dark hallway in the bowels of the courthouse parking garage. He ran down toward the end of the hall just as a fresh smoke bomb erupted in his face blinding him.

Help me see the way!

The sound of a struggle echoed in the distance. Celeste was calling his name. He followed her voice, praying with every heartbeat that he found her and that she would be all right. He sprinted down a hallway and up a flight of stairs. He'd found her once before, back in the farmhouse when the air was thick with smoke and his fellow US marshals had been fighting for their lives. He would find her now. He rounded another corner and then he saw her.

Celeste was being dragged along the hallway by the tall, bald man. There was something in his stance that Jonathan knew in an instant, even stripped of the wig, fake beard and glasses. It was Doppel-Dex. It was Dexter's half brother.

"Casper!" He pulled his weapon and aimed it directly at the man. "Stop right there and let her go, or I'll shoot!"

Casper turned and dragged Celeste around until he was holding her up in front of him like a human shield. He pressed a gun into the side of her head. She'd taken back the money his brother had stolen. She'd robbed him of his privacy. She'd exposed his identity and his crimes for all the world to see. Now he had her.

"You're not going to shoot me!" Casper

snapped. "Because if you so much as flinch, I'm going to shoot her first. You're going to turn around, go back and I'll let you know when I've decided where you can send the ransom money. I'm not leaving with nothing."

Jonathan whispered a prayer under his breath, raised his service weapon and centered the man in his sights. "Let her go and drop your weapon, or I will shoot."

"Do you really think you're fast enough and a good enough aim to make that shot without killing her?"

With Gott*'s help.*

Jonathan fired.

She heard the blast of the bullet, closed her eyes and felt a prayer move through her heart. Then she felt Casper's grasp weaken and release. He slumped to the ground.

"Thank You, God." She suddenly felt her knees wobble.

In an instant, Jonathan was by her side. "Celeste. Are you all right?"

"I'm okay." She pulled back a sob. "You rescued me."

He reached for her, pulled her toward him and brushed a kiss across her lips. Then he let her go. He turned toward the man lying bleeding on the ground and checked his pulse.

"He's still alive," he said. "His breathing is shallow, and he's going to lose consciousness. But if medical attention gets to him soon enough, he should live. Quick, find me something to help stop the bleeding."

She yanked off her scarf and passed it into his hand. He pressed it against the man's wound. She looked at him, this handsome, brave and incredible man trying to save the life of someone who would kill them both without a moment's hesitation.

Her fingers gently brushed against his shoulder. "You're incredible."

"I would've killed him, Celeste," he said. "Please don't doubt that. If I had to choose between your life and his…"

His voice trailed off as if too much emotion had suddenly choked the words from his throat.

"I know," she said. "You would have taken his life to spare mine. Still, you tried to find a way that nobody died. Not today."

He smiled. "Not today."

"Jonathan!" A voice rang out down the hallway. It was Karl.

"Down here! This way!" Jonathan called back. "We have one hostile down but alive. Requiring medical attention and to be taken into custody."

"And Celeste?"

"Safe and well!" Jonathan shouted back. Karl ran toward them, barking orders quick and sharp to whoever was on the other side of the walkie-talkie. Then he ended the call. "Is Stacy okay?" Jonathan asked.

"Minor injury." A smile of relief turned up the corners of Karl's lips. "Bullet just grazed her. She'll be fine. She's plenty tough. We're not sure if it was my bullet or hers that took Dexter Thomes down, but either way he's back in custody."

Thank You, Gott.

"Did you see my father and nephew?" Jonathan stepped back as Karl arrived, and let him take over.

"Last I saw they were helping evacuate people. Your dad said something about evacuating a barn."

"That sounds like him." He reached for Celeste's hand. They stepped away as what suddenly seemed like a crowd of officers, medical staff and others came running down the hall. Jonathan pulled her aside and moved along the hall until they reached a large window overlooking the snow outside.

"We only have a second," he said. His forehead wrinkled. "Not long. Karl is an incredible marshal and can take over for a few moments. But that's all we've got, seconds, and I don't know where to start."

"Then let me go first," Celeste said quickly. "I love you, Jonathan. I love how you think. I love how you question and how you search. I love how hard you wrestle with things. I love how deeply you care. And I don't know what happens next, but I feel like you're in my life for a reason, and I can't wait to find out what that reason is."

"I love you so much." He stared at her in amazement. "I never knew my heart was able to love anyone this way."

He brought his mouth down toward hers and she tilted her face up to his, and for one brief moment they turned their backs on the chaos around them and their lips met.

Celeste awoke the next morning to the sun rising high in the sky and the sounds of birds chirping outside the window. She stretched, feeling the warmth and comfort of familiar quilts around her.

There was a gentle knock on the door and then it flew back as Rosie ran in.

"You're here! You're really here! I thought it was a dream!"

Celeste laughed. "Yes, I'm here. It kind of feels like a dream for me, too."

Everything had felt surreal since the moment she'd taken the stand, being grilled by lawyers and having her sanity questioned, and then she'd looked out and met Jonathan's eyes. In that moment, everything had clicked, from what she'd seen in the data while scouring through the pages late at night to how she'd managed to see Dexter where he wasn't.

The answer was relationship. The answer was family.

"Mamm said you arrived in the middle of the night with two *Englisch* cops," Rosie said, perching on the end of the bed.

Celeste nodded. That was close enough. After Casper was arrested and she'd given her statement to the police, Jonathan had somehow talked Chief Deputy Hunter into letting them return home to the Mast family farm, as long as Stacy and Karl came with them. The two US marshals had driven in one vehicle while she'd ridden in the small church bus beside Jonathan, his arm around her shoulder and his hand tightly holding hers.

It was only for one night, just until they sorted out what would happen next and what needed to be done. But one night back in the Amish farmhouse, knowing she was waking up to see Jonathan in the morning, was already more happiness than she'd ever expected to have.

"An important *Englisch* lady is in the kitchen waiting to talk to you," Rosie said. She fidgeted slightly, holding out the fabric in her hand. "I was wondering if you wanted to wear one of my Sunday dresses. Mamm said you might want to wear *Englisch* clothes."

Bright yellow and pale pink fabric lay in her hands. Celeste smiled. "I would love to borrow one of your dresses, thank you."

For as long as she was in this family's home she would dress as one of them. She felt pretty adept at pinning her dress and cap on by now, but she was still thankful for Rosie's company as she got dressed. Then she followed the young woman down to the kitchen.

The beautiful wooden table had been transformed into a conference table. Stacy and Karl sat side by side, with Stacy's leg still in a splint from the bullet that had grazed her the night before. Jonathan sat on the opposite side, dressed as a marshal. At the head of the table was a striking woman, with keen eyes and graying black hair swept up into a bun. Everyone rose as Celeste entered.

She turned to Jonathan. To her surprise and disappointment, he didn't meet her gaze.

The woman stretched out her hand. "Chief

Deputy Louise Hunter," she said. "It's a pleasure to finally meet you."

"Thank you, it's great to meet you, too." Celeste crossed the room, took the other woman's hand and shook it. "What brings you here?"

"You." A smile crossed the chief deputy's lips. "I wanted you to know personally that Dexter Thomes and Casper Harrison have both been remanded into custody and prosecutors believe it's such a clear-cut case thanks to the evidence you've provided. We will continue to be vigilant about either Thomes or Harrison finding a new way to come after you and seek revenge. But I can't imagine law enforcement is going to allow either of them near a computer or unmonitored phone any time soon. And now that you've stripped them of the stolen money they have no way to pay for hit men. So, it's unlikely you will be considered an active target."

"I don't know what that means," she admitted. Again she tried to meet Jonathan's eyes, but he looked away, and the absence of his gaze dug at her as if someone was missing.

"It means that you're free to pursue other opportunities, another life," the chief deputy said. "And I'm here to offer you one. We have a secure facility in Colorado. It's both

home and office to a number of federal officers and support staff. We'd like to hire you
as an on-site data consultant. Your computer
skills and expertise are second to none. You'd
be safe inside our faculties in the unlikely
event someone should ever come after you, as
well as being able to use your skills to serve
your country."

It made so much sense. She wasn't an
Amish farm girl. She was a data analyst and
a computer programmer. She was an excellent
one. God had given her skills. She needed to
use them. Yet, as her eyes scanned the simple kitchen, with its wood-burning stove and
family table marked from hundreds of long
meals and conversations, she couldn't help
but think of all she'd be losing.

"Thank you," she said. "That's an amazing
opportunity. I need to think about it."

She crossed over to the back door, feeling
Jonathan's gaze on her. He stood. She tugged
on her boots, grabbed her cape and bonnet,
and stepped out into the snow.

She'd taken less than ten steps down the
path to the barn when she heard the door
swing open and shut behind her, heard Jonathan's voice calling her name. "Celeste!
Wait!"

She turned. There he was, running up the

path, with his straw hat and coat thrown over his *Englisch* clothes. She crossed her arms.

"You knew about this," she said. "That's why you wouldn't look at me."

"Of course I knew," he said. He reached for her hands. But for once she didn't reach back. Earnest eyes were locked on her face. "You're extraordinary, Celeste. You're so talented and incredible at what you do. You need to use those talents."

She stepped back and tossed her hands in the air. "Even if it means spending my life in a cement room, day after day, at a laptop... and without you?"

The last two words seemed to land and echo in the air.

Without you. Without you.

Something pained moved across his face. "But you're so good at what you do."

"I know." A smile crossed her face. "I am. But what if God is calling me to something more than that? Don't you want more for me?"

"What kind of more?" he asked.

He stepped in closer, but again she didn't let him take her hands.

"I don't know!" she admitted. "I just don't."

"Neither do I," he said. The side of his mouth curled into a smile. He stood there for a long moment, in the snow and early-morning sunshine, his face turned to her and his eyes on her face. "I'm still lost, Liebchen. But at least now I know I don't want to be lost without you."

He closed his eyes for a long moment. Then he nodded, as if hearing an answer or making a decision. He reached for her hand and she let him take it. "Come on, I need to ask my boss a question."

His hand tightened in hers. He led her back to the house and opened the back door.

"Chief Deputy Hunter?" he called. "I'd like to request heading up a trial project of US marshals who place needy and desperate people within Amish communities. It makes so much sense in light of the challenges posed by cyber warfare. We've learned from our experience with Dexter Thomes that few people look beyond the bonnet. The fact we'd be off the grid makes it harder to trace people. The friendliness of the Amish community is welcoming to outcasts and strangers."

Chief Deputy Hunter waited, looking from Jonathan to Celeste and then to their still-linked hands. Her gaze returned to Jonathan's face. "The idea has some merit. I can see it working well. Anything else?"

"There is," he said. She felt his hand tighten

on hers. "I can't do this alone. I'm going to need a civilian partner, someone who knows how to look out for threats and can analyze data. I want to suggest that you create a position for Celeste here, as well, where she can help support people placed in this program and do other data analysis as required for WITSEC."

She pulled her hand away. What was he saying? That he wanted her to stay with the Amish and join him in his work? Hope flashed in her heart. Did that mean he was opening the door to more?

"I think I'd be able to sell this idea to the higher-ups," Hunter said. "On the condition we create secure cover stories for you both, and also create a secure data facility perhaps disguised as a barn or other building, where you have access to cutting-edge technology. Are you interested in taking on that kind of job, Celeste?"

To live with the Amish but continue using her skills to help people? Yes, her heart knew its answer. Yes, this was what she wanted very much. She glanced at Jonathan. "Can I talk to you for a minute?"

"Sure." They stepped back outside.

"You told me some Amish use electricity and technology in their places of work, but not at home, right?" she asked. He raised an eyebrow, but nodded. "I'm only taking this job if I can still maintain that kind of balance in my life. I'm not going back to being online 24/7. I want all the cutting-edge technology WITSEC would supply me with to stay in the office. I want to live the *plain* Amish life outside of work hours."

"I understand and I think I can get Hunter to agree to that." A smile curled on his lips. "I want to go back to living like the Amish, too. But I'm not going to become baptized, so I can stay in law enforcement. Now I have one more important question."

He dropped to one knee in the snow at her feet. Her breath caught in her chest.

"I know where my heart is calling me, Celeste," he said. "It's calling me to you. It has been ever since the moment we first met and I know with every beat of my heart that it'll always keep calling me to you. I know it's sudden, but I don't want separate lives and cover stories for us. I want one life. One story. Together. So I'm asking you, please marry me, Celeste. Be my wife, share my home, share my family and build on it with children of our own."

The happiness that filled her heart was greater than she'd ever known, but when she opened her mouth she found just one word tumbling out. "Yes!"

"Yes?" He leaped to his feet. "Did you say 'yes'?"

"Yes!" she laughed. "Yes, I will marry you, Jonathan. Yes, I will join your family and raise our children near the Amish. Yes, I love you and my heart feels called to join with yours."

"Thank You, God!" A prayer crossed Jonathan's lips. Wrapping his arms around her waist, he pulled her tightly to his chest. She felt his heart beating against hers. Then he kissed her, deeply and lovingly, holding her securely in his arms until they heard David and Samuel banging on the window, calling them in for breakfast.

* * * * *

*If you enjoyed this story,
look for the other books in the
Amish Witness Protection series:*

Amish Safe House
by Debby Giusti
Amish Haven
by Dana R. Lynn

Dear Reader,

About how much time a day do you spend on the internet? If I'm not careful, I can easily spend hours surfing the web until I end up feeling grumpy about just how much time I've wasted. But I've also made some amazing friends online and use the internet to stay connected to people I care about.

Some of the most wonderful people I've met online are fellow writers. I often get together with authors on Twitter to write together and keep each other motivated. There are fellow Harlequin authors like Anna Adams, who has written for Superromance and Heartwarming, and Danica Winters, who writes for Intrigue. There's L. E. Wilson, who writes paranormal books and whom I finally got to meet in person while I was on vacation last year, and fledgling author Rachel Berros, who's still awaiting her first sale. We even have authors join us from overseas, like Anne Marie Stamnestro in Oslo. I am very thankful for the encouragement and friendship they bring to my day.

Writing about Celeste and Jonathan really made me think about how I use technology, especially when it gets in the way of spending time with those I love. I hope you enjoyed this story and are able to find balance in your own life, whether you're reading this in a paper book or an electronic reader. Thank you again to all the amazing readers who've gotten in touch through email and written letters. I really enjoy hearing from you!

You can find me on Twitter, @MaggieK-Black, or at www.maggiekblack.com.

Thank you all for sharing this journey with me,
Maggie

Get 4 FREE REWARDS!

We'll send you 2 FREE Books plus 2 FREE Mystery Gifts.

Love Inspired® books feature contemporary inspirational romances with Christian characters facing the challenges of life and love.

FREE Value Over **$20**

YES! Please send me 2 FREE Love Inspired® Romance novels and my 2 FREE mystery gifts (gifts are worth about $10 retail). After receiving them, if I don't wish to receive any more books, I can return the shipping statement marked "cancel." If I don't cancel, I will receive 6 brand-new novels every month and be billed just $5.24 for the regular-print edition or $5.74 each for the larger-print edition in the U.S., or $5.74 each for the regular-print edition or $6.24 each for the larger-print edition in Canada. That's a savings of at least 13% off the cover price. It's quite a bargain! Shipping and handling is just 50¢ per book in the U.S. and 75¢ per book in Canada.* I understand that accepting the 2 free books and gifts places me under no obligation to buy anything. I can always return a shipment and cancel at any time. The free books and gifts are mine to keep no matter what I decide.

Choose one: ☐ **Love Inspired® Romance**
                Regular-Print
                (105/305 IDN GMY4)

☐ **Love Inspired® Romance**
   Larger-Print
   (122/322 IDN GMY4)

Name (please print)

Address   Apt. #

City   State/Province   Zip/Postal Code

Mail to the Reader Service:
IN U.S.A.: P.O. Box 1341, Buffalo, NY 14240-8531
IN CANADA: P.O. Box 603, Fort Erie, Ontario L2A 5X3

Want to try 2 free books from another series! Call 1-800-873-8635 or visit www.ReaderService.com

---

*Terms and prices subject to change without notice. Prices do not include sales taxes, which will be charged (if applicable) based on your state or country of residence. Canadian residents will be charged applicable taxes. Offer not valid in Quebec. This offer is limited to one order per household. Books received may not be as shown. Not valid for current subscribers to Love Inspired Romance books. All orders subject to approval. Credit or debit balances in a customer's account(s) may be offset by any other outstanding balance owed by or to the customer. Please allow 4 to 6 weeks for delivery. Offer available while quantities last.

Your Privacy—The Reader Service is committed to protecting your privacy. Our Privacy Policy is available online at www.ReaderService.com or upon request from the Reader Service. We make a portion of our mailing list available to reputable third parties that offer products we believe may interest you. If you prefer that we not exchange your name with third parties, or if you wish to clarify or modify your communication preferences, please visit us at www.ReaderService.com/consumerchoice or write to us at Reader Service Preference Service, P.O. Box 9062, Buffalo, NY 14240-9062. Include your complete name and address.

LI19R

2018 LOVE INSPIRED CHRISTMAS COLLECTION!

You'll get 1 FREE BOOK and 2 FREE GIFTS in your first shipment!

This collection is guaranteed to provide you with many hours of cozy reading pleasure with uplifting romances that celebrate the joy of love at Christmas.

YES! Please send me the first shipment of the 2018 Love Inspired Christmas Collection consisting of a FREE LARGER PRINT BOOK and 3 more books on free home preview. If I decide to keep the books, I'll pay just $20.25 U.S./$22.50 CAN. plus $1.99 shipping and handling. If I don't cancel, I will receive 3 more shipments, each about a month apart, consisting of 4 books, all for the same low subscribers-only discount price plus shipping and handling. Plus, I'll receive a FREE cozy pair of Holiday Socks (approx. retail value of $5.99)! As an added bonus, each shipment contains a FREE whimsical Holiday Candleholder (approx. retail value of $4.99)!

☐ 286 HCN 4330　　　　☐ 486 HCN 4330

Name (please print)

Address　　　　　　　　　　　　　　　　　　　　　　Apt. #

City　　　　　　　　State/Province　　　　　　　　Zip/Postal Code

Mail to the **Reader Service:**
IN U.S.A.: P.O. Box 1867, Buffalo, NY. 14240-1867
IN CANADA: P.O. Box 609, Fort Erie, Ontario L2A 5X3

READERSERVICE.COM

Manage your account online!

- Review your order history
- Manage your payments
- Update your address

> ### We've designed the Reader Service website just for you.

Enjoy all the features!

- Discover new series available to you, and read excerpts from any series.
- Respond to mailings and special monthly offers.
- Browse the Bonus Bucks catalog and online-only exculsives.
- Share your feedback.

Visit us at:
ReaderService.com